Critical Praise for *The Freedom Artist* by Ben Okri

"With the stark power of myth, this political allegory evolves into an argument for artistic freedom." —*New York Times Book Review*

"A perfect read for a post-truth era." —NPR

"*The Freedom Artist* . . . can be read as a kind of revision of Plato's allegory of the cave, in which art, rather than offering distracting illusions, can tap into foundational truths and help us free ourselves from the prison of existence. The concise, declarative prose and the parable-like architecture of the stories resemble ancient forms of wisdom literature." —*Wall Street Journal*

"Man Booker–winner Okri's modern allegory specifies and beautifully renders the impact on the human spirit when people are deprived of history and truth. Written with a striking simplicity that belies the significance of its message, Okri's tale is especially resonant in our current post-truth environment."

—*Booklist*, starred review

"[H]aunting and inspiring . . . In this story of political abuse and existential angst, Okri employs a powerful and rare style reminiscent of free verse and evoking a mythical timbre. This is a vibrantly immediate and penetrating novel of ideas."

—*Publishers Weekly*, starred review

Prize–winning Okri writes a passionate cri de coeur, a clarion call to activists everywhere to resist apathy and recognize that we are all on this beautiful globe together and that it is ours to lose."

—*Library Journal*

"*The Freedom Artist* is a fable-like allegory set in a dystopian future in which the 'Hierarchy' is dominant, the citizens trapped and muted, except sometimes when they are heard screaming in their sleep. It is through this world that Karnak must travel to find his lover, who has been arrested for asking the question: 'Who is the prisoner?'"

—*Literary Hub*, one of the Most Anticipated Books of 2020

"*The Freedom Artist* represents a heady jumble of influence and inspiration, a tapestry of biblical reference, mythology, folklore, and fable. The lyrical simplicity of Okri's prose, with its short sentences and chapters, only heightens the power of the novel's political message."   —*Financial Times*

"A multilayered allegorical narrative that cuts to the heart of our current political and cultural malaise, while maintaining a mythical, mesmeric flavor that makes the reader feel these are stories they have always known . . . It's savagely political, disturbing, and fiercely optimistic, the deeply felt work of a writer who refuses to stop asking the hardest questions."   —*Guardian* (UK)

"Just as you're thinking, 'So this is what Dave Eggers's *The Circle* would be like if it were written by a poet,' Okri slips you a shot of ayahuasca and things get decidedly freaky and apocalyptic . . . A beautiful and timely appeal for the importance of books, subversive stories, and love." —*Times* (UK)

"A meditation on the threat to freedom represented by the emergence of what is already called 'a post-truth society' . . . It's a novel for our times." —*Scotsman* (UK)

"The book posits the theory that we are all in an inescapable prison . . . The novel is written in a postmodern style reminiscent of Henry Miller or William Burroughs." —*i*

"Okri creates a chilling atmosphere in *The Freedom Artist* . . . [His] rhythmic, folk tale–like prose is beguiling." —*Sunday Times* (UK)

"Ben Okri's most significant novel since his Booker Prize–winning masterpiece *The Famished Road*, *The Freedom Artist* weaves together ancient myth and modern politics for an impassioned story primed for the post-truth age. A story of love and loss, fiercely told and impossible to ignore." —Waterstones, one of the Best Books to Look Out For in 2019

"*The Freedom Artist* has a compelling power and energy that won't let the reader go." —*Herald* (UK)

PRAYER
FOR THE
LIVING

BEN OKRI

BROOKLYN, NEW YORK

Published by Akashic Books
All rights reserved
©2021 Ben Okri

Hardcover ISBN: 978-1-61775-863-8
Library of Congress Control Number: 2020935824
First published in the UK by Head of Zeus Ltd.
First Akashic Books printing

Akashic Books
Brooklyn, New York
Twitter: @AkashicBooks
Facebook: AkashicBooks
E-mail: info@akashicbooks.com
Website: www.akashicbooks.com

To Maggie McKernan,
for the care
and the years

Read Slowly

Table of Contents

It is vain to do with more what can be done with less.

WILLIAM OF OCCAM

Boko Haram (1)

They strapped the bomb around his chest and buttoned up his shirt. His father was with them. When the boy looked up at him, his father smiled. Together they recited the words of the prophet.

The father stood there and watched as they led the boy away. He prayed that the boy would be brave and would do what he had been told. He knew the rewards in paradise were great. He could see the rewards already.

At the marketplace they let the boy go. He wandered a few steps and looked back. They stared at him brightly. Then he walked unsteadily past the fish sellers and the cloth merchants and the women who sold provisions on a cloth on the floor. Some of them knew him and called out to him. But he went on walking. He looked steadily ahead. Sweat formed in beads on his forehead.

He went to the center of the marketplace, where it was

busiest. As he walked he recited the words they had taught him. They were not words from the Koran. They were words given to him by the men from the sect. He recited the words in the heat and noise of the market. Then he stood in the center and waited.

He did not know what he was waiting for. They had only told him that when he was in the center of the marketplace he was to wait. He was not to look at anyone. He was not to speak to anyone. He was only to recite under his breath the words he had been given.

He did not know about the scattered fragments of limbs and the ripped earth as the bomb tore up the marketplace. He did not know about it because he was still saying the words he had been given when it exploded.

Prayer for the Living

We entered the town at sunset. We went from house to house. Most of the roofs were shattered, the walls blown apart. Everything was run-down and deserted. The town quivered with death. The world was at the perfection of chaos. Gunrunners lived off the desolation. It was as expected.

The little godfathers who were in control raided the food brought for us. They sabotaged the airlifts and the relief aid. They shared the food among themselves and members of their clan.

We no longer cared. I had gone without food for three weeks.

I feed on the air and on my quest. Every day, as I grow thinner, I see more things about me. I see the dead. I see those who have died of starvation. The dead are happier than we are, living their luminous lives as if nothing has happened. They are more alive than us. They are everywhere.

The hungrier I become, the more I see them. I see my old friends who have died before me, among a chorus of flies. They feed on the light of the air.

They look at us, who are living, with pity and compassion. I suppose this is what the white ones cannot understand when they come with their television cameras and their aid.

They expect to see us weeping. Instead they see us staring at them with a bulging placidity in our eyes. We do not beg. Maybe they are secretly horrified that we are not afraid of dying this way.

But after three weeks of hunger the mind no longer notices. One is more dead than alive. It is the soul wanting to leave that suffers. It suffers because of the body's tenacity.

2

We should have come into the town at dawn.

In the town everyone had died. The horses and the cows and the goats too. I could say that the air stank of death, but that wouldn't be true. It stank of rancid butter and poisoned heat and raw sewage and flowers.

The only people who weren't dead were the dead. They were joyful and they sang lovely songs in low enchanted voices. They carried on their familiar lives.

The soldiers fought eternally. It didn't matter to them how many died. All that mattered was how they managed the grim mathematics of war. All they cared about was winning the most important battle of all, control of this fabulous graveyard, this once beautiful and civilized land.

3

I was searching for my family and for my lover. I wanted to know if they were dead or not. If I didn't find out, I intended to hang on to life by its last thread. If I knew that they were dead and no longer needed me, then I would die in peace. All the news led me to this town.

If they are anywhere they are here. This is the last town in the world.

Beyond its broken gate lies the desert.

The desert stretches all the way into the past. It stretches into history, into the western worlds. It extends to the source of drought and famine, to the mountains of lovelessness. From its peaks, at night, the grim spirits of negation chant soul-destroying songs. Their songs steal hope from us and make us yield to the air our powers. Their songs are cool as mountain rain and make us submit to the clarity of dying.

Before all this came to be there were all the possibilities in the world. There were opportunities for starting from small things. There were all the chances to create a new history and a new future, if only we had seen them. If only we had taken them.

But now only the songs of negation lie ahead.

4

We search for our loved ones mechanically. We search with a dryness in our eyes. Our bellies no longer exist. Nothing exists except the search.

We turn the corpses over, looking for familiar faces. All the faces are familiar. Death has made them all my kin.

5

I search on.

I come across an unfamiliar face. It is my brother.

I nod.

I pour dust on his flesh.

Hours later, near a dry well, I come upon the other members of my family.

My mother holds on tightly to a bone so dry that it wouldn't even nourish the flies.

I nod twice.

I pour dust on their bodies.

6

I search on.

There is one more face whose beautiful unfamiliarity will console me. When I have found that face then I will submit to the songs of negation.

7

Night was approaching when I heard a different singing. It

came from an unfinished school building. It was the most magical sound I had ever heard. I thought only those who know how sweet life is can sing like that, can sing as if breathing were a prayer.

The singing was like the joyous beginning of all creation. It was a holy yes to the light in all things, the light that makes the water shimmer, that makes the plants sprout, that makes men and women gaze in wonder at the radiance of color, the emerald of the sea, the silver of the stars.

It was the true end of my quest, the music to crown this treacherous life of mine. It was the end I couldn't have hoped for or imagined.

8

It took an infinity of time to get to the school building. I had no strength left. It was only the song's last echo, resounding through the spaces of my hunger, that sustained me.

After a vast cycle of time, during which history repeated itself and brought about the same results, because we never learn our lesson, never love enough to learn from our pain. After maybe a century, I finally made it to the door of the school.

But a cow, the only living thing I saw in the town, went in through the door before me. It too must have been drawn by the singing.

The cow went into the room, and I followed.

9

Inside, all the space was taken up with the dead.

But the air didn't have death in it. The air had prayer in it. The prayers stank more than the deaths.

The dead here were differently dead from the corpses outside.

10

The dead in the school were, forgive the paradox, alive. I have no other word to explain their serenity. They had made the room holy. In their last moments, they had thought not of themselves, but of all people who suffer.

I did the same thing. I crawled to a corner, leaned against the rough clay wall, and found myself praying for the whole human race.

I knew that prayers are possibly a waste of time. But I prayed for everything that lives, for mountains and trees, for animals and streams, and for human beings, wherever they might be.

I heard the anguished cry of all mankind, its haunting music as well.

11

Without moving my mouth, for I had no energy left, I began to sing. I sang in silence. I sang all through the night and I sang into the dawn. When I looked at the body next to me and found the angular unfamiliarity of its face to be that of my lover, I sang all through the recognition.

I sang even when a white man with a television camera came into the school building. I sang while, weeping, he filmed the roomful of the dead for the world to see. I hoped he recorded my singing too.

12

The dead were all about me. They were serene.

They didn't urge me on. They were just quietly joyful.

They didn't ask me to join them. They left it to me.

What would I choose? Human life, full of greed and war and selfishness. Human life, low in awareness, dim in its light, judgmental, unforgiving, uncaring. Human life, gentle, sometimes wonderful, sometimes kind. But human life had betrayed me.

Besides, there was nothing left in me to save. Even my soul was dying of starvation.

13

I opened my eyes for the last time. The cameras were on us. To them, we were the dead.

14

As I passed through the agony of the light, I saw them as the dead. They were marooned in a world without pity, without love.

15

The cow wandered about in the apparent desolation of the room. It must have seemed odd to the people recording it all that I should have made myself so comfortable there.

I did.

I made myself comfortable.

16

I stretched out my hand and took the hand of my lover. Her hand was cold and dry. With a painful breath and a gasp and a smile, I let myself go.

The smile must have puzzled the journalist.

If he had understood my language, he might have known it was my way of saying goodbye.

An Inca Elegy

I had taken a group up into the mountains to where the last of the Incas lived. The Inca women up there in the forest are the most beautiful you are ever going to see. I had just come out of the army then. The army was good for me. But for a while it made me a brute.

As I was taking this group of Americans through the village I came upon an adobe house. It was the only one I had permission to take the tourists through. I knocked and went in. They speak Quechua up there. I had learned Quechua in the army. I showed the tourists how the last of the Incas live. It was a room just like this one here in Machu Picchu. In one corner they have their vegetables, in another their traditional stove. High up they have their dried fruits and their hay. Even their rooms are terraced. I was amazed at how much they could fit into those small rooms. They had everything they needed in there.

As I was showing the tourists around I noticed this Inca woman in a corner. The adobe house belonged to her. She stood there, peeling a dried fruit. There was a terrible sadness on her face. For some reason it pierced deep into my heart. Like I said, I speak Quechua.

"Does our presence upset you?" I said to her.

"No."

But she still had the sadness.

"If we have offended in any way, I wish to apologize now. We have no desire to offend you at all."

"You have not offended me."

"Have any of these tourists offended you?"

"No."

"Because if they have, I will speak to them immediately and they will apologize."

"They have not offended me."

"Maybe our being here in your private space is an offense, for which I sincerely apologize."

"It is not an offense and there is no need to apologize."

The immeasurable sadness was still in her eyes. I could feel it and it cut me to my soul. I could not continue the tour. She stood there in a corner and the sadness was like the weight of centuries. I kept puzzling in my mind what might have caused it. The thought would not let me rest.

"What is it that troubles you? Are you sick? If you are sick, tell me. I have all kinds of medicines with me. You can have them all."

"I am not sick."

"Is it money you need? I don't have much, but you can have all that is with me."

"It is not money."

"Maybe it is family. Anything I can do to help, just ask me."

"Thank you. It is not family."

I was still racking my brains. I began to pace the room. Then she looked at me and all the poignancy of her sadness shot from her eyes into the foundations of my being. It rocked my heart, I don't know why.

She hadn't said a word. Then, as if overcoming a great struggle, she said: "The reason I am so sad is that I will never have children."

"Why not?" I said. "Of course you can. Look at you, you are beautiful and young."

She weighed me down with her eyes. "Have you noticed anything about the village?"

I came out with many things I noticed, but she kept shaking her head.

"There are no men," she said.

I hadn't considered it but I had noticed it. It was true. There were no men in the village.

"Where are they?"

"They go to the cities for work. They never come back."

I had heard about this. I did not know why this prevented her having children.

"Don't worry. I am a man," I said passionately. "I can

marry you. I will marry you now. We can have children."

She gave me a long look. It was disquieting. As she looked at me I felt myself fading till I was almost a shadow. I don't know how that happened. Before, being in the army, I had a strong sense of myself and my presence. I knew who I was. But under her gaze I immediately felt my identity dissolve. I have no idea why.

"What is your name?" she asked.

I told her my three names. She repeated my last in an undertone, with a little smile.

"From your last name I can tell you have Spanish blood."

It was true. I have a small amount of Spanish blood, from my great-grandfather.

I couldn't see the bearing it had on our discussion.

"I can't marry you," she said, lifting up her eyes as if she saw through the roof of her adobe house to something bright and iconic in the mountains.

"Why not? I am a man."

"You are not of my blood. You are not pure. I can only marry a man with pure Inca blood."

"But why?"

"That is how it is. That is how it has been for a thousand years."

"But all your men are gone. They're in the cities. You said yourself that when they go to the cities they don't come back."

"I know."

"I am a man. Marry me and have children and your sadness will vanish."

She smiled for the first time. But the smile was somehow sadder than her sadness.

"I can't. That is how it is. For a thousand years that is how it is."

"But what will you do? Would you rather have no children or children with someone like me? Can you not change a little?"

"I can't," she said.

Then with a slight movement of her shoulder, the conversation was over. She was very beautiful. I stood there speechless for a while. Then I felt a veil descend between us. It was like the coming of night in the mountains. It comes suddenly as you are walking the trail. The next moment, if you are not careful, you walk right off the edge of the mountain. That's how it came between us. I could not see her anymore through the veil she brought between us.

Somewhat broken, I concluded our tour. As we left I said goodbye to her. She stood still in the corner and did not move. She did not respond to my farewell.

Why am I telling you this? I don't know. But this room here on Machu Picchu is just like the room we were in. It reminds me of her. It brings back to me all the force of her sadness. I can feel it now.

Please excuse me. We shall resume our tour. I'll be back shortly.

A Sinister Perfection

She had always wanted a doll's house. As soon as she was old enough, Hyacinth asked her parents for one. Her mother was doubtful; she thought it would distract her daughter from real life. Her father felt it could provide a useful education in running a house. He was so taken with this notion that he had a doll's house commissioned at once.

He wanted it to be gigantic and the exact replica of their own house on Baker Street. His precise instructions required a fiendish architect. When it was delivered, he found its replication perfect in scale and detail. Hyacinth was so fascinated that she spent hours comparing it with the original.

She spent most of her time making the doll's house as like their real house as possible. She filled it with her imagination. She slept and woke in one of its rooms. In another of its rooms lived Mum and Dad. The kitchen below, the servants' room at the back, were all living places in her mind.

It occurred to her that what happened in the doll's house had a magical effect on what happened in the real house. When she wished someone to be ill in the doll's house, someone fell ill in the real one.

She continued in this game till one day she imagined a stranger paying a visit to their house. She imagined him a peddler of stones and magic lamps that she had read of in books. Then a week later such a stranger, just like the one she had imagined, knocked on their door. He stood in the gaslight, a peddler of blue stones. The servants were about to send him away, but Hyacinth begged her father to let him in. He had piercing eyes and wore a red turban. He was from Kazakhstan and had walked the Silk Road. When he stepped into the living room and saw the doll's house, he said: "It is just as I dreamed it."

"What on earth do you mean?" her father said.

"I had a dream of such a house."

"Do you mean the doll's house?"

"Yes. Your daughter summoned me here. I have come. What do you want of me?"

"Can you make the little house come alive?" Hyacinth asked.

The stranger turned his fierce blue eyes on her. "The little house lives!" he said, placing a blue stone in Hyacinth's palm.

Before the father could protest, the stranger was gone.

* * *

From then on the doll's house teemed with invisible activity. Little beings lived and fretted in there within its lighted windows. Hyacinth listened to the whispers in the little house till her eyes grew red with exhaustion. At night when everyone was asleep she would steal downstairs and pay keen attention to the muted activity in the house. Often she would be found asleep in front of it and would be carried back to bed without waking. She began walking in her sleep, stealing downstairs to where the real life was, in the doll's house.

In her dreams, she was the mistress of the house. She gave orders to an army of servants. In one dream her father was in jail. In another her mother was banished to the country. She would wake up horrified. Not long afterward bailiffs came to the house and arrested her father on charges of financial irregularity. Her mother fell on a riding trip in the country, broke her ankle, and was confined to bed for several weeks.

Hyacinth had the big house to herself. She didn't think for a moment that the doll's house had anything to do with these unhappy incidents. Now that she was mistress of the house, she succumbed to its power and her character changed. She became imperious.

One night the invisible beings invaded the real house. She saw them filing out of the little house and she screamed. No one believed her. She grew hysterical and the servants locked her up in her room till they could get the doctor out to look at her.

During that time the invisible creatures occupied the big house. They roamed about in the pantry. They clambered about in the living room. At night Hyacinth could hear them whispering about fire.

"With a divine fire," she heard one of them say, "we'll burn down this house."

"And in three days it will be rebuilt again."

"By the Architect."

"With his runes."

"Which he studies while the world burns."

"Out of the ashes the great house will rise."

"And the young girl will have learned her lesson."

"Yes, the lesson of perfection."

That was when it occurred to her that their house had become the doll's house, and that their lives were in peril. She called out to the servants, she tried to warn them, but they would not listen. She heard them whispering in the corridor. She could have sworn they were drunk.

That night something caught fire in the pantry. The blaze spread. There is no need to say that the house was burned down, and that they were ruined. There is no need to state either that when the house burned down only the doll's house, in its sinister perfection, remained miraculously intact. No one knows what became of it.

Her father was released from jail. The charges against

him were found to be ridiculous. Many suspect the charges were trumped up by rivals who envied his success.

They moved to a small house in the country. Her mother sold off all her horses and never rode again. Her father learned to read and interpret runes. Day after day, Hyacinth waited for the stranger to return, so she could give him back his blue stone.

Ancient Ties of Karma

a stoku

It was a clear bright day. Two men were about to fight a duel. One had a long knife. The other had a short sword curving sharply at the end. The one with the knife was younger, cockier, and wild. He was very sure of himself. The one with the curved sword was older, more civilized, and did not want to fight. He had done everything to avoid it. But the younger man forced his hand.

They had the first of their duels.

It began in a flash. One made a move, the other ducked, and the younger plunged the knife into the older man's chest. This was in a shadow realm.

Then the friends traveled on. They walked through many landscapes, traversed many cities. Outside a railway station they had another flash fight. The one moved, the other ducked, and the younger one planted the knife in the older one's chest. This was in a realm of thought.

The two men, bound together by mysterious ties, journeyed on. Traveling together had not resolved the bad blood or the fated mood between them.

The day of doom arrived. Fate had given them time to overcome their differences, and they hadn't. The older one never provoked. He was bound to the younger one by ancient ties of karma. They came to a village in the woods. It was near a cemetery. They were now in real time.

The younger one provoked, and attacked. The older one ducked, and desultorily stabbed his weapon at the younger one who made an evasive movement. Then he planted his long knife deep into the belly of the older man and watched the blood pour out. This was real.

The younger one was not satisfied with his victory. He was outraged at the older fellow's poor technique. While the older man stood with the knife sticking out of him, his blood draining to the ground, the younger one gave him a master class.

He replayed their moves triumphantly.

"You made a thrust. I moved sideways. The knife went between arm and body. Then I delivered the coup de grâce."

But then the older man suddenly came to life. He made extraordinary movements, faster than the wind, swifter than thought. He made three slashing cuts and brought the sharp, curved end of his weapon down on both sides of the younger one's neck, without touching him.

They were master strokes. The older man could have killed the younger man whenever he wanted. It became evident that the older man was the master all along. He had deliberately refrained from killing the younger man.

Then something bizarre happened. Events in the real world caught up with the truths of the shadow world. The younger man fell as if he had been struck fatally. He fell against the wall. As he sank to the ground, he cried: "Hell has opened for me."

Right next to him a monkey's head, yellow and red, projected from the wall. The younger man let out a barely audible Don Giovanni wail as he was snatched down to the underworld.

The older man, accompanied by the melody of the stars, was swept up to heaven.

Dreaming of Byzantium

. . . and gather me
Into the artifice of eternity.

W. B. YEATS

For a long time he had been trying to go to Byzantium. He had started the journey many times. For twenty years, he had been setting out at the same time of year. But whenever he set out the journey always became complicated. On one occasion he found himself in another city without knowing how he got there. The journeys took on a life of their own. They took him not where he wanted to go, but where the journeys themselves wanted.

The desire to go to Byzantium represented to him something of an impossibility. Every year he would get out his maps and study all the routes by which to get there. He dreamed of long train journeys, considered walking, and was even tempted to try the obscure method of being borne there by birds. Nothing seemed too excessive for accomplishing a task that fate had made difficult.

The years passed and the journey had not been made. He had amassed a collection of photographs and drawings, paintings and lithographs and engravings. He had read poems and travel journals, sought out travelers' tales and ancient legends. He had approached Byzantium as one approaches the stories of a famed kingdom beyond seven mountains. Only rare travelers return from it with gold-rimmed eyes. He had approached, but had been unable to find the gate by which to enter.

Every poem he had read about it was a closed castle, every drawing a hieroglyph, and each traveler's tale a riddle. He had begun to think that Byzantium existed in a separate world, a world of blue dragons and topaz lions.

He had kept his hopes for this journey to himself. He never demeaned his dream by telling it to anyone. Byzantium was his secret destination. He felt in some ways that it was his destiny.

2

Many years ago he had actually received an invitation to go to Byzantium. It was as if fate wanted to tempt him with that which he sought but could not have. He was invited to be on a panel of image interpreters. The letter of invitation had puzzled him. Its formality, its circuitous language, made it seem as if it were addressed not to an individual, but to a group. He responded to the letter diligently and awaited a reply. A date had been given for the conference, which was to take place in the ancient capital, on the shores of the Bosporus.

He thought that at last the closed gate of his dream was beginning to open, that the fates had been appeased. He had fallen under the spell of an ancient legend. There is a place that each person cannot go to. And if they do, a mysterious fate awaits them. Everyone has a Paris inaccessible to them, a Rome they will never arrive at, a forbidden Lagos. The key to that place is held by one of the three sisters of fate.

The invitation seemed a sign that the key had been turned in its lock. He dreamed of white swans on the bright river. Once he dreamed of a black swan and awoke perplexed. What might happen to him now the spell was broken?

Places that we have failed to get to exert a profound fascination. It could be the next village, a museum in the city, an alleyway just off your street. Or a letter one is waiting for that never arrives.

That they never replied to his letter, or that their reply got lost in the post, only confirmed that the key opening the door of his destiny had not really been turned. He waited weeks, then months, for a response. He wrote several times. He heard nothing. It was as if fate were playing a game with his fondest hopes. But the game fate played only deepened his desire.

Desire increases in direct proportion to obstacles preventing its fulfillment. Some might think that the desire is the obstacle. None of this crossed his mind. When the opportunity to visit Byzantium faded, he went back to making plans, studying maps, and consulting ancient books in libraries about the weather there. Byzantium became a living place in his imagination. Is there anything more real than what we have created in our minds, with all the power of our imagination and ignorance?

Every day he went to this place that was on the margins of his mind. This place existed alongside his daily work, his everyday tasks. At night he inhabited this realm. He dwelled in its markets and its mosques, its parks and its cathedrals. He wandered on the roads that led to the river. The muted evening light over the city and the eastern origins of its language became his constant delight.

All he had to do was shut his eyes and he was there again. It was what he looked forward to most. For months he lived like this, in the two realms. His daily life meant less to him than his dream life. As his daily life grew more confined, this dream life acquired more liberty. Slowly he became a shadow in the city where he lived. The world ceased to notice him. He passed into daily insubstantiality. But in his dreams he acquired form and body and freedom.

He developed growing mastery of this secret domain.

As he lost the city of the day, he gained the city of his dreams.

3

One day he had gone for a walk in his neighborhood, along the canal, in West London. It was an unusually cold day and at the end of the walk he had taken refuge in a café. At that time of day the café was usually empty. Steam from a coffee machine misted the windows. He took a seat near a window and stared out into the misty world. He liked the world misty. He liked the world unclear.

While he had been sitting there, his mind empty, a man had come into the café and taken a seat at the table next to him. After a while the man addressed him, in a voice that had the hollow quality of a cave.

"I see that you like the world misty," he said.

"I do."

"Too much reality, eh?"

"The world seems unreal."

"What is real for you?"

"Far-off places that I cannot get to, dreams more real than fire."

"So you too are haunted by unattainable dreams?"

He turned to look properly at the stranger. He noted the darkness of his eyes and the strangeness of his dress. He wore a blue-red robe and a gold-fringed turban and white shoes that curved upward at the tip. He seemed like one who had come from a place where the air is of fire and where the eyes see nothing but stone. His face was hard and sculpted like rocks in wild places. From his robe came the elusive odor of the desert and of eastern marketplaces. From his eyes came the hint of unpredictability.

"Why do you say that?"

"I recognize the curse of those who are trapped in their dreams."

"How can you recognize it? What do you do? Who are you that you can say such things?"

The stranger was silent. He had the air of a wandering magician. He could even have been a wizard. It was those piercing eyes. They saw through illusion. The stranger laughed. He had good teeth.

"What I do does not matter."

"What matters then?"

The stranger smiled, got up, and with deliberate motions put on his white gloves. Then he left without another word. When the stranger left, the mood of the café was different. It was muggier than before.

He sat at the window, no longer looking out. The window was no longer misted.

4

Every now and then we meet someone who seems to have the solution to that which perplexes us. We sense they have the solution even before they have spoken. It is as if they are the key that the universe has sent us. He sensed from their only meeting that the stranger might be his key.

He went back to the same café, and sat at the same window, hoping to meet the stranger again. He had many questions for him. He waited at the same place, and at the same time, for weeks. Before he sat down and ordered his cup of tea, he knew he would not see the stranger that day. Each day he knew it. He knew it sometimes by the shapes that formed on the misted windows. Sometimes he knew it from the vacant mood of the café, even when the café was full.

It is said that certain people, with the force of their charisma, change the mood in a room. They don't have to be important. They might appear insignificant. Do certain people foreshadow their arrival? Even the most skeptical people, going for a walk, have sometimes had the sense of a friend they have not seen for a long time. They turn a corner and there, at a bus stop, stands the friend. Do we sometimes sense people before we meet them?

Each day he knew by the mood of the café that the stranger would not appear.

Weeks went past in this way. The world changed quietly. The headlines on the newspapers spoke of distant wars that were creeping closer. One headline started a mild disturbance in him all day. They were setting up a colony on Mars. One hundred people had been chosen for a one-way journey to the red planet. On the day he read the news story he was at the café, staring through the misted window, nursing a cup of tea.

He had a sudden feeling. When he looked up, the mood of the café had changed. There was a blue quiver in the air. He sensed but could not see it.

At the next table sat the stranger. He was wearing white gloves. There was a faraway look in his eyes, as if he were looking beyond the veil of the world.

5

He had not seen the stranger come in, and had not noticed when he sat down.

"Are you still haunted?" the stranger said in a dry voice.

"Yes."

"I thought so."

"Why?"

"Unreality makes the world."

"Unreality?"

"Yes."

"I thought reality made the world."

The stranger smiled. Deep grooves appeared on his face. An uncanny light shone in his eyes. "Unreality makes reality."

"I don't follow."

"You have not understood the power of your dreams or the gift of your obstacles," the stranger said, a dark gleam in his eyes. "If fate shuts a door on you, it is because it wants you to find a greater one. The normal door you want to pass through is not for you. Every obstacle presents us with a magical solution."

The stranger paused. There was a momentary silence in the café, as if everyone were listening.

"You have been defeated by reality," said the stranger, after a while. "The only way to defeat reality is with unreality."

"How do I do that?"

The stranger was no longer listening. Now he had the solemn face of a tribesman of the steppes. "If you will trust me implicitly," he said, "I will show you the power of your dreams."

"You have my implicit trust. I am at the end of my tether. I will try anything."

"Good," the stranger said, leaning forward. "Now look into my eyes. While looking think of what you dream about most."

He looked and felt the world about him dissolving.

"Deep in my eyes you will see a flame and a sword. You must choose one. If you choose the sword, wield it. If the fire, hold it aloft."

He looked deep into the stranger's eyes. He saw a sword and a flame.

"Have you chosen?"

"Yes."

"Reveal your choice to no one."

"Not even to you?"

"Not even to me."

"All right."

"Now go home and we will see what happens."

When he blinked, the world was misty. When the mist cleared, the stranger was gone. There wasn't even a cup on the table where he had been sitting.

6

He went home and read. He felt out of sorts. He felt a little unlike himself for the rest of the day. It was a feeling he couldn't get rid of. In the evening a curious malaise stole into his limbs. He went for a walk to try to shake it.

The edges of buildings, flocks of birds, the spikes of metal fences, quivered lightly in his vision. Back home the corners of the room bothered him. It seemed to expand in ways that were impossible. That night, unusually for him, he fell into a sudden deep sleep. He had hardly touched his head to the pillow when he was encompassed by the dark.

The next morning he woke in an alien bed. The room was new to him. He had the curious feeling of having been transported to a world that was mildly familiar. The walls of the room were of a dazzling whiteness. On the wall opposite him there were two floor-to-ceiling mirrors. Between them was a large slender television. There was a white chaise lounge near the bed. The ceiling was fretted with a simple abstract design composed of intersecting lines.

A woman was working on a small black computer on the solid mahogany table. She was beautiful, in an unfamiliar way.

"Who are you?" he said, raising himself on the pillow.

The curtains were still drawn and a soft darkness pervaded the room. The oblique light of dawn crept around the edges of the curtain.

"Darling, you're up?" The woman smiled at him. "You have been sleeping now for twelve hours. I didn't want to trouble you."

"But who are you?"

"Darling, stop playing silly games. What are we going to do today?"

She had stopped working on the computer. She stared at him with cool eyes. He decided to go along with the pretense for a while. He studied the woman. She had red hair, full breasts, was not young and was not old. When he looked across at what she was doing he saw, to his surprise, that she had begun to fill out the spaces of a drawing. She sketched the shape of a minaret, with people in the background, and pine trees scattered in a small park.

"You're an artist?"

"Of course I am, silly. What's wrong with you today?"

"Where are we?"

She stared at him hard. She stared at him a long time. From her gaze he perceived that if he continued like this she might consider something drastic. He sat up in bed and rubbed his eyes, to give the impression that he was the victim of a persistent sleep.

"We're in Istanbul," she said, concluding her long scrutiny. "Do you remember now?"

"Yes, of course," he said lightly, frowning. "Istanbul, you say?"

"Yes, dear, Istanbul." She gave him another look. "What shall we do today?"

"If we are in Istanbul, where are we staying?"

"You are being strange today. You must be tired. Or forgetful. I hope you're not going to get worse. Raffles, dear. We're in Raffles. You chose it. Maybe you need a bit more sleep."

He hid beneath the sheets. He passed from thought into sleep. When he woke, the curtains were drawn back and he saw a distant river. He got out of bed and went to the window. It was an excellent view. He could see a long bridge and on the other side houses on a sloping hill. The houses were white and ranged with charming symmetry. Their red-tiled roofs made a fine pattern.

On the lower terraces of the tower next door there were the last traces of snow. As he looked across the city he saw snow on rooftops and on lawns.

He turned away from the window. The woman was still drawing at the table. He went past her to the bathroom. The floor and walls were of marble. There was a bathtub and a separate shower and a large clear mirror over the washbasins. The doors were of smoky glass.

"Did you know we have our own butler?" the woman called out from the other room.

He contemplated answering but decided on silence.

"Well, we do. She's very nice."

He had a quick shower while pondering the luxury of having a personal butler in a hotel. As he dried himself it occurred to him to ask whether he had any clothes with him. It was all so strange that he had no idea what he had and what he hadn't. He came out of the bathroom wrapped in a towel. Outside the bathroom door he saw a closet. In the closet were open suitcases. In one he recognized his own clothes. There were also shirts and coats on hangers, and on the floor his favorite old slippers. He put on black corduroy trousers and a blue shirt and went back into the room.

"This came earlier," the woman said, handing him a note.

The note was from the concierge. He was due to meet one of the hotel staff at 11 a.m. to go through an itinerary of places he wanted to visit in the city. All this was new to him. He looked across at a clock on the bedside table. It was 9:10 a.m. In that same glance he saw the stack of books he had been reading at home. It reassured him to see them. Made him feel less unmoored.

"Shall we go down to breakfast, dear? I'm starving."

The woman stood up and put a wrap around her shoulders. She picked up a black handbag and key card. He followed her mutely. Outside, there was a finely wrought table on which was a brass bowl. It looked valuable, like an antique. There were paintings all along the walls and the floor was of marble. Hanging from the ceiling was a cocoon of pearls forming intricate curves.

"You could wear that as a dress," the woman said, admiring the exotic chandelier.

The lift arrived and they got in. He stood at a distance from her, in a corner. He wanted to get a good look at her. She had a very fine figure. Her face had clean lines, her jaw almost classical. When she turned her eyes on him, he noticed they were green, like a tiger's. Her gaze was piercing, cold, but kindly. The more he stared at her, the more familiar she became. She bore his scrutiny calmly. Not a word passed between them.

When the lift came to a halt, he stepped out into a white corridor with a shining marble floor. He was careful not to slip. On the wall there was an abstract mosaic, made of tiles, behind glass. There were framed drawings along the white walls.

At the end of the corridor was the vast lobby, with long-stemmed flowers in giant vases on glass tables. Sofas and little tables formed interlocking semicircles. They passed a recess where three managers sat at desks behind their computers. They leaped to their feet.

"Good morning, sir," the senior among them said. "I trust all is to your liking?"

"Yes, thank you," he said, a little thrown by their attention.

"Is there anything you need?"

"Not right now."

"And you, madame?"

"No, thank you."

"Is the room comfortable?"

"Very."

"We are pleased. If there is anything you need at all, just tell us and we will do our best to accommodate you."

"Thank you," he stammered.

He was not used to this quality of politeness and concern, and at first it disconcerted him. The staff were polite and kindly all the way to breakfast. By the time he had taken his seat he felt a little more comfortable.

The breakfast room was spacious and white and clean. There were gigantic flowers on a huge central table. They sat near the big windows. He watched two soldiers patrolling the grounds outside. There was snow at the foot of trees. The steel-and-glass tower reflected the sun from its hundred silvered windows. He looked around the room. There was a large family at the round table next to them.

He settled his gaze on the woman who sat opposite him. She looked startling in her cool beauty.

"What is this name they call me?"

"It's your name."

"My name?"

"Yes."

"How do they all know my name?"

"It's part of their training."

"Their training?"

"Learning the names of guests."

A waiter appeared at their table like a genie. They gave him their orders. He followed their complicated requests. She wanted a yogurt, Bircher muesli with soy milk, and white tea. He wanted muesli with fruit salad and orange juice to start. Then he wanted a full English breakfast with two eggs. They ate silently. He often felt her eyes on him. But when he looked up, she turned away.

7

At eleven they were in the lobby. He stood near a table, on which were golden cups, vases, a metal dish, filigreed lanterns, all in an ancient Arabian style. Before him, on the massive central wall, was a vast photomontage of the Dolmabahçe Palace. The photograph somehow simultaneously depicted the inside and the outside of the palace, with its labyrinthine steps, its balusters and halls, its rooms and stairways, its tapestries and crystal chandeliers, its peacock on a red rug and its Mongolian tiger. The more he stared at the picture the better he felt. It was a vertiginous work, and it reminded him of the rigorous symmetries of Escher.

While he was contemplating the paradoxes of the stairways in the picture, a slender woman appeared before him.

"My name is Nergis," she said. "And it is a pleasure to have you with us, Mr. Oraza. Shall we sit?"

They sat down on one of the light-colored sofas. The lobby was spacious, the ceiling high, and the chandeliers elaborate. Behind them were two giant sculptures. One was of a seated woman.

Nergis had a notepad in her hand. She looked at him. "I thought we should discuss things you would like to see in Istanbul."

"So we are in Istanbul?"

"Yes," Nergis said, looking at the woman as if to ascertain whether he was serious. The woman shrugged.

"My husband has a strange sense of humor," she said.

Nergis smiled. "There are so many things to see in this city that it would take you months to see them all."

As she finished, a lady with a bright smile came to their table and asked if they wanted anything. He was hesitant, and Nergis suggested Turkish tea. The serving lady returned a short while later with a silver platter bearing dark-red teas in small transparent glasses. There were also two bottles of ice-cool water and a bowl of sugar.

He was not sure how to drink the tea till the woman put two small cubes of brown sugar into her glass. Then she stirred and sipped. He did likewise. He was surprised by the bitter but delicate flavor. After the first few sips he felt mysteriously revived, but he didn't feel any clearer.

Nergis began asking questions about what they would

like to see. He mentioned one or two places that were famous. Nergis made notes and then suggested other places. The wife looked on with a half smile.

"I'd like to go where ordinary people live," he said.

"They live everywhere," Nergis said. "In Istanbul we have neighborhoods and each neighborhood has its unique character."

"What is your favorite neighborhood?"

"Beşiktaş. The bazaar."

"Put that on the list."

"And what are your favorite things to do in the day?" asked the woman.

"When I have a day off I love to go on the ferry along the Bosporus with a simit."

"Simit?"

"A bagel."

"I see."

"I love feeding the bagel to the birds. I love throwing pieces of bagel in the air and watching the birds catch them. Sometimes they feed off your hands."

"We'll do that then."

"I will put it on the list."

That's how they made the list. The serving lady brought Turkish tea twice and kept filling their glasses with water. When Nergis finished the list, she saw him staring at the photomontage.

"You like it?"

"It's intriguing."

"It was made by an American artist. It's a digital painting. The artist was given permission to photograph the Dolmabahçe Palace. Pictures of the interior and exterior are placed on the same surface. That is why a staircase leads to a red room and why . . ."

A concierge came over and whispered something to Nergis. When he left, she said: "Your car is here."

"Our car?"

"To take you on a tour of the city."

He looked at the woman. Her eyes shone but she said nothing. Nergis rose.

"I know you will have a wonderful day," she said.

"Thank you," he murmured.

A concierge led them through the revolving doors, into the sunlight where a black limousine was waiting. The woman who was his wife slid into the backseat, and he climbed in after her. The seats were plump. The driver started the engine. Then a man got into the seat next to the driver. He turned around to face them. He had sad eyes and a face that betrayed some hidden suffering.

"Welcome to Istanbul, Mr. Oraza. My name is Mehmet. I am your guide, and you are my sultan. Anything you want me to do, I will do."

The driver put the vehicle into gear and drove out of the hotel complex. As they drove out into the tangle of roads, he felt himself dissolving.

8

The window was the world and the world was misting over. A curious feeling that he was fracturing came over him. He shut his eyes. Instability returned when he opened them again.

They seemed to drive a long way around the city. Sometimes the traffic was light, and sometimes it was heavy. While they drove, the guide spoke. He weaved in and out of the guide's words, forming a mosaic picture of the city. The guide said it was a city of melancholy and dreams. Twenty-five centuries of history and five civilizations had been compressed into the city. It was the only city in the world that straddled two continents. The guide quoted an ancient chronicler, who said that if any city deserved to be the center of the world it was this one. It was a city of jewels scattered over seven hills. Jason and the Argonauts, seeking the Golden Fleece, had drifted through here. The streets had known the impress of Greek civilization, the Roman Legions, and waves of Ottoman Turks, who gave the nation its name.

"All who came here were changed by the dreaminess of the location. Four times the city has changed its name. And each of its names is a portal to one aspect of its dreams. Names are important here," said the guide, turning to stare at him.

"What do you mean?"

"To seek Byzantium is to seek a city hovering above this one, a legend half-lost among cathedrals and ruins. It is like seeking to live in a poem. No one who finds it escapes."

The guide stared at him. He withstood the stare. Then he turned to look out of the window, at the snow turning to slush along the roadside. He saw the pale white houses with red-tiled roofs. Trams weaving their way through the city put him in a thoughtful mood. He liked cities with trams. He gazed at storefronts, at cafés where people sat outside drinking tea in little cups. The sky was clear and a mild spring sun loaned the city its gold. He could tell by the names on signboards, and by the changing character of places, when he was passing from one neighborhood to the next. He saw mosques and churches and a cement-colored building, old before its time. Each mosque gave its neighborhood a unique mood. For a moment he thought he was in Egypt or Dubai. The feeling was elusive, but persistent. He stared at the roads, the towers, the flyovers, the shimmering glass of skyscrapers. He was seeing and not seeing, and he liked it.

The woman was silent beside him. She stared out of the window as if she were a part of what she saw. Maybe it was her way of being comfortable everywhere. Her gaze was detached and yet warm. Her detachment made her beauty more striking. But her face changed when she became aware that he was studying her. He could feel the invisible shield she was putting up against his scrutiny.

Outside, the mood of the sky doubled. He had been conscious of the silver mood of the sea without noticing it.

"The city is shaped by its rivers and its hills," said the guide. "I have brought you to the Marmara. Through these waters come the ships of the world. Do you see them? Then they have to go through the Bosporus, that narrow stretch of water, one of the most important gateways in the world."

He stared at the ships as the guide spoke.

"The ships go through it slowly. The ships you are seeing now are waiting their turn."

The car glided alongside the Bosporus.

"Beyond the Bosporus is the Golden Horn. The river divides the city. I will not give you its history or I will be talking for several weeks. The names alone are sometimes their own history."

He had stopped listening. The names had sent him off in a dream. He was no longer himself. He had gone off on the first of his slippages. He was now the sultan's palace with its centuries of Ottoman rule, its gold-leaf ceiling, its crystal-and-mahogany staircase, its magnificent carpets, and the room in which time is frozen, where Atatürk died. He felt the palace as a home of sighs and splendor. The gardens were full of whispers and the mirrors were full of songs. Its harems troubled his dreams. Its armed soldiers stood in constant vigilance. Its gate contemplated the Bosporus.

He would have continued in this dream but for his wife gently shaking his shoulder.

"Do you see the different heights of the wall?" said the guide. "That's because the sultan did not want the world to have a glimpse into his harem. So he built the wall higher here."

"How many wives did the sultan have?" asked the woman.

It was the first time she had spoken on the drive around the city.

"Sometimes they can have more than two hundred concubines."

Beyond the window the streets were throbbing. There seemed to him a strange contrast between the magnificence of the city, its domes, its palaces, its thousand spires, its beautiful mosques, and the crowds of people climbing the hills or hurrying along the streets.

Looking out of the window, on the Galata Bridge, it occurred to him that the city was a vast open museum, surrounded by a blue sea. They were in a traffic jam. The slowness of their crawl made him aware of a close line of men leaning over the bridge. They were looking earnestly over the waters.

"What are they doing?"

"They are fishing."

"What are they fishing?"

"Black Sea mackerel."

Then he saw the dark curves of their fishing rods. "I don't have a rod," he said wistfully, "or I'd join them."

"You can still join them."

"How?"

The guide asked the driver to stop.

They got out of the car. There was a chill wind blowing over the river.

They went among the men fishing. The men were solemn and silent and did not resent the intrusion.

"We keep a rod in the trunk of the car," the guide said. "Do you really want to fish? You could be here all day."

"Maybe another time," said Oraza.

They stood there and watched the swirl and flow of the water. The skyline was a music of mosques on the hills. While he stood there he heard the pern of a fishing rod spinning. None of the men caught any fish. They stood there patiently, as though fishing were an excuse for something more mysterious. He stood there with them and breathed in the essence of the Golden Horn.

After much driving around, after listening to the history of the city and the description of its famous sites, they were taken to a street of spices. There were small pyramids of yellow and red and gold beneath the wooden eaves of the market. The blended odor of peppers and turmeric was strong in their nostrils. The guide took them to a café and left them to themselves for a while. Oraza had red tea and the woman had black tea and baklava.

"I've wanted baklava all day," she said.

He noticed that her face had changed. Her features

were purer and whiter, her hair still red, her eyes still tiger-green. She was different but the same.

"Who are you really?" he said after a while. "I didn't want to ask in front of the guide."

"I am a dream that you had once and will have again."

"A dream I had once?"

"Before your obsession with Byzantium." A smile trembled on her lips. "If you like, I am the dream of Byzantium itself."

"How?"

"In the world in which you dwell, a castle can become a bird, a palace can become a song. This city is full of dreams and here dreams can become things. But things also can become dreams."

"I half understand you."

"There are many realities in this place. In which reality do you want to live?"

"Can I choose?"

"Of course."

He pondered this, his mind gently whirling.

"Those red and yellow spices, what do you think they might be?"

He looked at the mounds of spices and the men seated in the recesses of their shops. "I don't know."

"That is because you are looking."

"What should I do then?"

"Do what you do best."

"What is that?"

"Dream."

He let his mind drift and suddenly from the spices he was overwhelmed with the plangent sound of an old Turkish lute. He had heard it once before in his quest for Byzantium. The sound, like the sigh of abandoned lovers, brought a throb of tears to his heart. He gripped the table.

"Are you all right?"

He had no time to reply. The guide had returned and was urging them to continue the tour. Oraza discreetly wiped the tears from his face, and rose. The woman looked at him compassionately.

9

Outside, the guide said: "I want to take you to my favorite mosque."

They could see spires through stone arches. There was a clothes shop below. The guide led them up gray stone steps. When they entered the mosque, with their shoes off and the woman's head covered with an orange scarf, Oraza immediately felt the abundant peace of the place. The guide drew his attention to the Iznik faience tiles, with their intricate patterns of blue and yellow and brown on the walls and pillars. Light from the high-arched windows flooded the orange carpet. They stood beneath the circular low-hanging chandeliers and marveled.

"This is the Rüstem Pasha Mosque and it was built by

the great Ottoman architect Mimar Sinan in 1561," said the guide.

"I can see why it's your favorite mosque," said Oraza.

The dome with its patterns reminded him of peacock feathers.

"Come, let me show you something."

The guide led them out. They put their shoes back on and went down the stairs and out the back of the building. He showed them a stump of stone.

"That's where they chopped off the hands of women who committed adultery," the guide said dramatically. Then he added, "Or any other crimes in the old days."

The woman went over and, bending low, put her wrists on the stone, just to see what it felt like. They laughed nervously.

At a herbal shop on Asmaaltı Caddesi, they were served a red and refreshing tea. While they were drinking, the owner came in. He was a short, thickset man with a dense beard. When he saw Oraza, he said: "Have you found Byzantium yet?"

Oraza made no reply but studied the snake oil bottles and the argan cream and the leaves and the bars of Turkish delight patterned about the shop. The owner began telling them about the work he was doing with the distilled essence of herbs from all over the world.

"I have herbs here that cure cancer," he said energetically.

But Oraza was not listening because he was thinking

of the Byzantium he had not yet found. Then he had one of those moments of slippages. He found himself in a bazaar. Then he was in a shop looking at scarves and wraps. Then he was in a restaurant, drinking ayran. Then he had a vision of domes and spires against a deep-blue sky. Birds were circling the spires. All the while the guide was talking about the city.

When the slippage settled he was kneeling near a pillar in the Blue Mosque. It was crowded and there were shoes in wooden cabinets behind him. The woman was kneeling next to him and the Japanese visitors who went past took pictures of the two of them. The Iznik tiles gleamed in the muted luminous light from the Venetian windows. A moment later he put his palms to one of the four massive pillars called Elephant Feet. When he touched the pillar, he felt the charge of a dark tranquil light populated with forms and ghosts across the centuries who had made their pilgrimages to this place.

Outside, in the snow-covered park, they sat on a bench between the Hagia Sophia and the Blue Mosque, while the guide told them of the misunderstanding that led to the creation of the eight domes on the great mosque.

The day went fast but he tried to live it slow. The woman with him glowed in the sun. Sometimes she appeared small, other times she appeared tall. Sometimes her hair was blond, other times red. She too was a slippage, but she was always the same beneath her changing forms.

Later, when they were walking down the street, he saw an old wooden house with a black cat sitting on a window-sill. He felt again the instability of the world. All through a lunch of bluefish and salads the sense of unreality persisted. He was sitting across from the woman in the Balıkçı Sabahattin fish restaurant and she was telling him about her life in a narrative of spices and blue cloths. Her words turned into yellow birds in his mind. They were like the lost fragrance of golden incense.

They went across the Hippodrome and gazed at the Egyptian obelisk and the Delphic stone. Then they went down into the underworld and wandered among the columns and looked down into the dark waters. They encountered the two faces of Medusa. It was cold down there and in the water there were swarms of big dark fish. He felt, on touching a pillar, that he had seen an image of his future. But before he could grasp it they were above ground again and walking along the gray stones of the city walls.

Time kept breaking up for him. Some moments were long and sun-filled. Others were short and magical. There was a brief dream of the Jewish cemetery and a tramp sleeping on a bench and then wandering around in the splendors of the Grand Bazaar. He was next aware of trams grinding past them in the darkening street and then of their journey back to the hotel up in Zincirlikuyu, from where the city glimmered at night.

In the hotel lobby their butler hurried toward them.

She was compact and neat. She wanted to find out if there was anything they needed. All he wanted was a moment's rest before dinner. The butler had tea sent up to their room in an elegant tea service.

At dinner they listened to the gentle touch of the pianist performing Turkish songs.

"I can only be here when you dream me," the woman with him said, after they had ordered.

"What do you mean?" he asked.

"If you forget to dream me I won't be here."

"Why not?"

"It is the law of the world in which we meet."

"What are the other laws?"

"They are many, but really only a few."

"Give me one or two."

She thought a moment. They were sitting in a corner of the hotel restaurant, under a dim light.

"We are how we are because of how others are," she said quietly.

"That's hard to understand."

"It's very simple. I am how I am because of how you are. Mutually, we create our reality."

"I still need to think about it. Give me another."

"Each person, even those we love, suppresses some aspect of ourselves."

"Is that a law or an observation?"

"You will find that it is true here."

"Where is here?"

"The world in which we meet."

"Are there other worlds?"

"There are worlds in which we meet but don't know it."

After that they ate in thoughtful silence, nourished by a fine blend of Turkish red wine.

10

As his head touched the pillow, he went off into another slippage. The woman was no longer there. In her place was Bach's *Goldberg Variations*, played upon an invisible piano. Suddenly he was not himself any longer. He was a young English dancer who loved maps and was lost in the charms of the spice market. He was an Italian lecturer of semiotics sitting in a Bebek bar, staring at the Bosporus. He was a tour guide with a bad cold, conducting these demanding tourists through the labyrinths of the city. He was a fountain, lit at night, whose uprush of water failed to reach the night sky. He was an artist in Üsküdar, painting the same abstract canvas over and over again. He was the sarcophagus of Alexander the Great concealing a timeless secret. As if he were experiencing what the gnostics called the multiplicity and oneness of being, he was always something different and yet the same. But when he became the spice market, with its little pyramids of paprika and hibiscus, he fell into a long dreamless sleep.

11

He woke to find himself in the Hagia Sophia. He had no idea how he got there. The guide was not with them. He felt in the cathedral a great sense of spaciousness. A big section of it was closed off for repairs. He felt the woman with him, but he could not see her. She was with him in fragments of the Goldberg variation that was floating about him in the air. A sense of tranquility came over him. He wandered around on the ground floor. He gazed at the chandeliers. High above he saw the blue-and-gold mosaic of the Christ Pantocrator raise his right hand in gentle benediction, left hand bearing a golden book. On both sides of him, in roundels, were the Blessed Virgin Mary and the Angel Gabriel. There were verses from the Koran high up there too. The central dome had been taken over by Arabic calligraphy.

His guide suddenly appeared and told him, with the brevity of dreams, the legends of the Hagia Sophia. Here was the center of Byzantium. Here was once the center of the world.

12

He was wandering past a pillar when he saw the woman. She was on her knees, playing with the two black cats of the cathedral. As he approached, she looked up at him and smiled. She left off playing with the cats and joined him on his tour. They went upstairs and looked down over the nave. They were closer to the plaques with inscriptions.

They lingered at the blue-and-gold mosaics. They were in the Hagia Sophia a long time and were the last to leave. There was a mirror over the main door which reflected a fresco behind them. Each time he passed through a door in the cathedral he felt clearer.

It was sunny outside. They bought roasted corn from a vendor. The four minarets of the Hagia Sophia were like slender spacecraft about to launch into the cloudy sky. In Gülhane Park he saw water washing over the sculpture of a pink open book. Statues sat among the trees. Children were blowing bubbles next to a man who sold plastic pistols. There was snow on the grass.

13

He was getting used to being there. As they walked along the city wall, the woman changed again. She was now slim and tall. She was in an evil mood. She did not want to speak and she walked on ahead of him. When he caught her eye, the woman turned cold again.

They were looking for Hoca Paşa Sokak and they got lost. They went down streets with tramlines, past shops and cafés. They were misdirected several times. They found where they were looking for at the end of a street of restaurants. They stopped to have a bite in a small establishment. They had kalamata olives, grilled red peppers, and manti. Then they went to the Hodjapasha for the Mevlevi Sema ceremony.

Inside, the circular hall was crowded. The musicians came in with long white hats. He listened to the plucking of the yaylı tambur and the beating of the kudüm. When the dancers came into the center of the stage and took off their black cloaks, revealing the pure white coats and gowns underneath, he felt himself slipping. As they whirled to the rhythm of the ney and the kanun, and the mesmeric beat of the kudüm, he felt himself swaying and then rising. Soon he was lost in the immensity of Divine Love.

14

At dinner he was alone again. He was alone because of where the whirling dervishes had taken him. The waiter, solicitous and charming, was once a famous footballer. Oraza had a salad and minced lamb and a little red wine and went up to bed. He tried to sleep but he kept slipping off again. He was a Sufi dervish whirling through the universe and dreaming about a girl he once saw in a crowd. He was a waiter in Arnavutköy whose wife had left him after thirteen years because they could not have children. He was a film director in Tarlabaşı, a black and Gypsy neighborhood, looking for a long-lost friend. He was the Grand Bazaar with its shops of cloths and panoply of lights. He was the Hagia Sophia at night.

In the morning it was drizzling. The aria from the *Goldberg Variations* was in the air again. He listened to it while he looked at the sprawl of houses across the city. The city had become the music. He stared at the bridge outside his hotel window. Beyond the Bosporus white houses with ocher tiles ranged along the rhythm of the hills.

Downstairs in the lobby, the doorman got him a taxi to take him to the Eminönü pier. He wanted to visit the Asian side of the city. There was mostly a dark-haired crowd in the ferry waiting hall. The men were bearded. After a while he began to recognize the Turkish configuration of face. How do people acquire that characteristic stamp of national features on their faces? he was thinking. Then among the faces he saw one that was different. She was singing softly to herself by the window. When she looked up, he saw that it was the woman who claimed to be his wife. He went over to her.

"I've missed you," he said.

"You can't have missed me or I would be there."

"Sometimes I forget how to dream," he said.

"Last night you lost me and did not notice."

He could not speak.

"Do you know how strange it is to not be the center of your loving attention?"

He stayed silent.

"It makes one disappear. It makes one invisible."

In a far corner of the waiting room a woman was practicing tango steps to music in her headset. He slipped into someone's mind and did not know how. It was a man thinking of his girlfriend. That morning he realized he could not live with her. He realized also that one morning he would commit suicide and it would never be clear why he had done it, because all the evidence showed that he should have been happy. He was still in this man's mind when the ferry arrived. He looked around to see who it might have been. All the young men had anxious faces. It could have been any one of them.

They got on board the ferry and made their way to the top deck. He watched the ships drifting on the Bosphorus. He watched the churning of water in the ferry's wake.

15

When he looked sideways he saw the woman in a haze of hovering birds. In a kind of benediction, she was feeding them. The wind was strong and cold. In Kadıköy they came upon the statue of a man with a plate of fish. It was raining now and they bought transparent umbrellas. That day it seemed the woman enjoyed laughing at him. When he made a mistake, when he opened the umbrella and dropped it, she laughed.

They caught a yellow bus to Bağdat Avenue and walked its length and sat in the drizzling park. He had lowered his umbrella, to feel the rain on his face. He was happy. She did not speak, but her face glowed.

Near the pier, they wandered through the market of spices and fruits. They came to a secondhand bookshop and spent an hour browsing downstairs and upstairs. They bought an old book about the city and another on Sufi dancing. In the Çiya Sofrası restaurant opposite they sat at an upstairs window and looked at the busy street. They had İskenderun kebabs and a mixed salad and black tea.

"Why do you speak so little?" he said to the woman.

"It's better to listen."

"What do you listen to?"

"The city."

"What do you hear?"

She fastened on him a luminous gaze. "I can hear a woman thinking that it is easier for her to love someone she does not know."

"Really?"

"Yes."

"What else can you hear?"

"I can hear a widower thinking that we meet people late in their personal story and that's where the difficulty of love comes from. What can you hear?"

"I can hear a student thinking that we fall in love with a woman's face and are often disenchanted with the character behind it."

"Many women are thinking that too about men."

"Some survive the disenchantment and discover true love."

"True love can only come after disenchantment."

"Why is that?"

"The first enchantment is a madness and a fragility. The madness of a fool and the fragility of a spring flower. The second enchantment is as slow as the growth of a great tree and deeper than the ocean. But to get to the second enchantment one must survive the desert and the fire. Then one must grow a new heart, for the first heart dies with the disenchantment."

He stared at her as she spoke. Her eyes were far away and shone like green diamonds.

16

They had finished eating. They had paid and were going down the narrow stairs when he heard himself say: "Will you marry me?"

She laughed. "I'm your dream. How can you marry your dream?"

17

At 6:35 p.m., just outside the restaurant, just after she mentioned the word dream, the chain around his neck broke. The seven jewels fell down his chest. One by one he fished them out from under his shirt.

It was dark over the marketplace. He knew that it was time to go back home.

18

As they were leaving Kadıköy, on the ferry, he saw two flags fluttering on the dock. They passed the silent shipyard. As they approached Eminönü he saw, high up on a street, traffic like lava pouring down the hill. Another street was like jewels tumbling from a height. He watched the slow crawl of pearls across the bridge.

In the night the steeples levitated in gold. The hills unveiled their minarets.

He felt the flight of cathedral melodies and the weight of the tunes of the mosques. The city haunted him with its history and its nocturnal splendor. The night hours flowed by and the long age bloomed in ruins and towers. The city at night was a carnival riot of red and blue and yellow lights, glimmering bulbs of diamond and gold.

19

Back in the hotel they lingered in the heft and lightness of the lobby. They went upstairs and decided to have a hammam. He was struck that the woman who looked after them was called Ebro. He slept briefly in a paradise of bubbles. Back in their room he found it hard to sleep. He kept falling into slippages. He suffered and was resurrected in the march of the centuries. Like flowers, the palaces sprouted. The cathedral drew the heart of the world like pilgrims to a center. The two cities rose and became one, with the curve of its river and its emerald skies. He became the viaducts and the underground cistern and the dark water shivering with big dark fish. He could not sleep and that aria pervaded his sleeplessness. Then at last he embraced the aria and realized that the music had coded the city for him privately. He was drifting now when he felt the strange woman next to him and he wanted the music played over and over again the way some people would like to see, in a special light, the face of their elusive dream of love brought fresh from the living air.

20

At the point in which he was happiest, he became the city itself. He became its pavilions, its golden throne, its sycamore trees, and the shimmer of the Bosporus in the sunlight. And when he became the city he lost everything. He fell into a long mysterious absence, and woke up in his own bed, surrounded by stacks of books about a city he had never visited.

21

Two weeks later he was sitting by the misting window of the café. He had been back there every day and the strange man had not returned. In the newspapers he had learned that during his absence three young girls had fled to Istanbul on their way to join a violent Islamic cult in Syria. There had been a diplomatic row.

He had been sitting by the window, thinking that the man would never return, when the lights changed. He turned and saw the strange man next to him, dressed in white and wearing white gloves.

"What did you do to me?" he said to the man. "Was that a dream or was it real?"

"I can buy you a ticket to Istanbul and when you come back you can tell me which is more real."

"But what did you do to me?"

"I showed you that it is unreality that makes the world real."

"I don't understand."

"You take every day for granted. That for you is real. But if you stop taking it for granted it becomes unreal. Unreality makes the world real. If you remember how unreal the world is you will be fine."

22

One day, three months later, he was wandering the streets of a northern city. He had never felt clearer in his head.

As he was walking he heard the slender strains of the aria from the *Goldberg Variations*. It was seeping out of a fine building. Without a moment's thought he went and knocked on the door. No one answered. He pushed the door open into a clear space with polished floors. He saw couples practicing salsa. Farther on he saw a ballet class in progress. There was a woman at the piano. When she looked up, he saw that it was her.

What do you do when your dream has stepped out of your dream?

The Canopy

a stoku

I had gone looking for them in the hotel where they were staying. I had just arrived. They were in their room. I wanted somewhere to sleep. I thought of big beds with clean white sheets. In the hotel lobby tables were being laid out.

I took off my trousers and coat and hid them overhead on a tarpaulin canopy. Then I met a senior waiter who was carefully moving tables to their new positions. I asked him about it. He was keen to explain. He said there is a perfect geometry of tables which creates optimum pleasure for guests. Too close to one another and they irritate. Too far from one another and diners feel isolated. It's a kind of magic. He showed me. He placed one table at a distance from another, and asked me to observe the mood. It was quite fascinating. He had a point.

While he was speaking I noticed he was wearing something odd on his chest. It was the smooth furry face of a wolf. It projected outward from his chest.

"What's that?" I said.

"What do you think?"

"It's a wolf."

"No it's not!" came a voice from behind me.

I turned and saw a boy with his mother. She had a big face.

"No it's not," said the boy again. "It's more like a girl."

I looked back at the waiter. I was surprised to see that he now had the brightly colored face of a girl around his neck. The wolf on his chest had gone. What had happened to it? Then I wondered what he meant by having around his neck the face of a girl done in brightly colored dots. It occurred to me that perhaps he was sexually ambiguous. I'm not sure why. It was a silly thought. After all, he was the master of the magic spacing of tables.

He turned back to his work. I went back the way I had come, and retrieved my trousers and jacket from their hiding place on the canopy. In the corridor beyond I put on my trousers. The waiter was watching me getting dressed in the corridor.

When I was putting on the jacket he asked what I thought I was doing.

"What do you mean?" I said.

"What are you playing at?"

I looked puzzled.

"I saw that," he said, pointing at the canopy.

I tried to explain it all to him, but the other waiters had gathered. For a moment I thought he was going to throw me out of the hotel and ban me from ever being a guest. But somehow I got out an explanation. I had some friends staying there. I was hoping to find them. I needed to sleep, but I was fine now. They heard me out. I must have talked for a long time. I must have told them a very long story indeed. I got lost in my story and wandered down the many corridors of my own feverish invention.

When I finished, time had altered. I had talked myself into a blue space. There was no one around. The corridor was empty. I went out to the lobby and waited for my friends to emerge from the world of sleep.

In the Ghetto

We were returning from a visit to a relation and had just turned off Badagry Road into the dusty street that led home, when our old white Peugeot spluttered and fell silent.

We piled out. The doors were hot and the side windows reflected the glare.

The smell of heated oil came from below.

The road burned through our shoes. The sun was fierce overhead. Kiosks and stalls quivered in the light. A black dog lay beside a water tank. Women selling cooked beans and fried plantain sat on both sides of the road. The blare of highlife music pouring out from the record shops increased the force of the heat.

Dad lifted the hood of the car and peered into the engine. We stood around, trying to avoid the eyes of old men sitting in the shade of beer shops, young men loafing, girls who paused in their chores. Their eyes looked at you as if you were a fool. We felt foolish standing around the broken-down car in the middle of the ghetto.

I went to see what Dad was doing. He looked up at me briefly, his glasses catching sharp rays of light. Sweat dripped down his forehead. He had taken his coat off and his armpits had circles of wetness.

He checked the oil, tweaked the plugs, and tried the ignition. The car wouldn't start.

"We'll have to push," he said.

The heat from the car stunned us. Apart from Dad, there were just three of us. We were kids and we felt defeated. A dog ran past, and barked at us. We were the ghetto entertainment.

The three of us pushed the car, but it would not move. We gave it another try, and still it would not move. On the street, bits of broken glass shone like points of fire.

People went past and glanced at the stalled car. Men in khaki trousers and dirty white shirts, men in shokoto and multicolored shirts, men who were barefoot in shorts went past and none of them stopped to help. A family of women, a mother and her several daughters, paused to talk about the car. We were sweating as we watched them. They did not sweat. Their faces were like smooth petals of hibiscus flowers in the sun.

When they went, Dad said: "Boys, you have to push this car or we'll never get home."

Home was not that far away. It was less than two hundred yards. Dad could not afford to leave the car because it would be picked clean by the time he came back for it. There were no mechanics around. We had to push the car home or lose it.

We pushed again, but it did not move an inch.

"Ask people to help you," Dad said.

We asked passersby. We asked the big men, the young boys, the men loafing in the shade of drinking parlors, but no one would help us.

Uri, the middle boy of us three, said: "People just don't care." He was the one interested in engineering. He looked at the people who went past with a sour expression.

"Let's not care about them. Let's push," Essay, the youngest, said.

He was defiant, and tried pushing on his own. The car didn't budge. He gave up. We watched the ghetto silently watching us. A white cat gazed at us from the top of a rusted, abandoned car. A woman selling soft drinks eyed us from the roadside. She gestured to me to come and buy her Fanta. I shook my head. Dad lit a cigarette in the driver's seat and began smoking. We watched the smoke plume out from the side window.

"No one is going to help us," Uri said.

"They might."

"Why don't we ask those girls?" Essay said.

"You ask them and see what they say." Uri's voice was thick with irony.

"Are we just going to stand here?"

"What else do you suggest?"

"It's very hot."

"Get in the car then."

"My feet are burning."

"Stop whining."

"I'm not whining."

"Shut up, you two," I said.

"I'm thirsty."

"He's thirsty."

A group of girls came toward us. They were pretty and all dressed up in party clothes. The girls scrutinized us as they drew up to the car. Uri pretended to be looking into the trunk.

Essay stared at them and said: "Will you help us push the car?"

The girls stopped and walked around the car and saw Dad finishing his cigarette. They talked among themselves. Then they took off their high-heeled shoes and all six of them began pushing the car lightly while laughing. We joined them in the pushing but their laughter robbed us of effort. The car didn't move and they gave up and dusted the soles of their feet and put their shoes back on, laughing and teasing us about how handsome we all were. Then they wandered off into the heat-shimmer of the dusty road.

When they had gone, Dad said: "Who were those girls?"

"Nice people," Essay said, "who tried to help."

"They were making fun of us," Uri said.

Our shadows were sharp and dark on the rough dirt road. Dad got out of the car and fiddled about with the carburetor some more. His hands came out dirty and he wiped them clean with a rag he had in the trunk. The ghetto had not stopped looking at us. A group of urchins gathered under the eaves of a shop, watching us. In the same shop an old man smoked a cigarette and drank a bottle of beer. He studied us with rheumy eyes. The charcoal seller had piled out his charcoal in bags and sat with his wife under a tattered umbrella. They stole glances at us.

Even a curled-up dog kept an eye on us.

"What are we going to do, Dad?" Uri said.

"What else can we do? We'll push."

"But it's only the three of us," Essay said.

"I will help you," Dad said. "I will push from the driver's door. If it kick-starts, I'll jump in."

Dad opened the driver's door and he pushed with the door open. We all heaved at the car from behind. For the first time it moved. It moved a few inches and we heaved harder and the car started a little up the road. When it had gained some momentum Dad jumped into the car and worked the throttle and gears. The engine whined, cranked, groaned, then died out.

"That was good," Dad said.

He rolled up his sleeves. We pushed again, Dad with

the door open, and us at the back. We got the car rolling past the charcoal sellers and Dad jumped in, the exhaust spluttered, the engine caught, and then petered out.

"We're nearly there. Keep going, children!" Dad said.

We were exhausted. The metal of the car gave off a burn. Fumes from the exhaust mingled in our breathing. More eyes watched us from the shade along the debris-ridden road. A motorcycle roared past. On its pinion was a slim girl in a short skirt, without a helmet. She looked back at us and smiled.

"I'm tired, Dad," Uri said. "Can I have a Fanta?"

"You will all have Fanta when we get home. First we have to get the car to start."

We stood around. Uri had his arms crossed. Essay stared at the boys who were watching us.

"Why are they looking at us like that? WHAT ARE YOU LOOKING AT?" he shouted.

All along the road those who hadn't noticed us before noticed us now. More eyes watched us and Essay went and sat in the backseat of the car.

"What are we going to do, Dad?" he asked.

"We are going to get this thing moving."

"How? No one will help us. All they do is look."

"People always look. When you are in trouble, they look. People like looking. Don't let it worry you. It's what you do that counts, not whether they are looking."

"But why don't they help?"

"People never help when you need them."

"When do they help?"

"When you don't need them."

"But that's bad, isn't it?"

"That is the world, Essay. When you don't need them, they will rush to help. When you need them, they are never there."

"Why is the world like that?"

"I don't know."

"What can we do?"

"You must learn to do things for yourself. Don't rely on others, or they will let you down."

"What do we do now?"

"We push."

"Just us?"

"Yes. We push as if we are the only ones left in the world."

"Okay, Dad."

Essay got out from the backseat. We both began to push. Essay groaned and shouted as he pushed. We both heaved and put our backs into it and drove our feet into the ground and the metal of the car burned our backs. We dashed our rage against the heft of the car. Then slowly the earth shifted beneath our feet.

Uri joined us and he too was heaving. Dad got out and pushed from the open door and we got the car moving a little. We kept on, shoving and getting up a run. Dad urged us on. We went past the Coca-Cola kiosk, the tire sellers, the barbers, and the hotel where the prostitutes sat in the shade fanning themselves.

The car was rolling along now and we kept up the run. Dad delayed getting into the car. He urged us to go faster and faster. We were not tired anymore. The car was on the move. Before we knew it we had to jam up closer to one another because all of a sudden several hands had joined in the pushing. We got up a big momentum and the engine growled and cranked into life. The exhaust coughed, and the car sped away from us, and we were left running along the road with only the air in front of us.

When we ran to catch up with the car we saw a crowd of men and boys and little girls with us. They were all smiling. Before we could thank them they melted back to the roadside, to their kiosks and their trades and their loafing. Only a little boy in ragged shorts stood there in the middle of the road waving at us.

Dad eased into gear, and drove us home.

Hail

I was at the framer's. It was a cold day with a wan light in the sky. I had come in from the cold because I wanted frames for my pictures. I'd been thinking about this for a long time.

I had been walking down the street when I saw the heavy stack of Victorian frames neatly arranged in the shop. I had made a good find.

My daughter was asleep in her soft lambswool blanket. My girlfriend had stopped in a shop to buy some honey. I stood in the warmth of the framer's shop looking out of the big window. I wanted to surprise my girlfriend when she came hurrying out of the honey shop. I waited for a long time.

The framer was busy with a couple. They were taking quite some time buying a light wood frame and some nails and grips. The young man talked volubly to the framer while

I waited. Then my girlfriend went past with an anxious look. She could not see me or the pram along the road.

Then she caught a glimpse of me in the framer's window and smiled and came in. We waited patiently together. The young man began telling a long story about an aunt who found a painting in the attic. The framer was very obliging in the way he listened. We stood there a long time and the light in the sky darkened a little.

I had my back to the couple. My girlfriend was looking out of the window. That was when I heard the young man's girlfriend say: "George, how many paintings have you sold?"

"Five hundred," he said.

"Five hundred?" said the framer.

"Five hundred," said the young man.

"That's a lot of paintings," said the girlfriend.

"Five hundred," said the young man, "and then I gave up."

"You gave up? Why did you give up?"

"It's complicated. I was getting depressed. It was very hard. I got seriously depressed."

"But still, five hundred paintings!"

"I was getting very seriously depressed. It was hard."

"Very odd that you gave up after selling five hundred paintings."

"Not really. I was depressed. I was worse than depressed."

There was a pause. They were silent. It began to rain outside. You could hear the patter of rain on the window. It was as if someone dimmed the light of the sun.

"All the painters I met who are in their sixties look terrible. They're all a mess. They are the unhappiest-looking people I know," said the young man.

He paused.

"I got unbelievably depressed," he added.

I looked at him. He didn't look very depressed now. Though you never can tell. He was buying a cheap frame not for a work he had acquired, but for a painting his girlfriend's mother had found in her basement. They'd had it valued, but it wasn't worth anything at all. They were having it framed anyway.

The framer was very helpful. He offered to carry the frame to the car, but they wouldn't let him.

I caught another glimpse of the young man as they went past the big window. He didn't look depressed. He had a careful three-day growth of beard. His beard was not depressed either. But you never can tell.

We watched the hail drumming down on the pavement.

Mysteries

"Do you know we have two bodies?" said the poet.

"Two bodies?"

"One visible, the other invisible."

They were sitting in a restaurant, waiting to be photographed for a charity event in a theater. The actor turned to the poet and registered his existence. It was as if he had been invisible and his utterance had rendered him visible.

"How so?"

"Think of the amputee."

"What about the amputee?"

"They feel the missing limb."

"There is a scientific explanation for that. Something to do with nerve endings."

"The invisible limb outlasts the visible one."

"But does it feel?"

"If we have two bodies, it follows that we have two brains."

"Two brains?"

"The visible limb feels through the visible brain, and the invisible limb feels through the invisible brain."

The actor stared at him skeptically.

"The invisible brain could rightly be called the mind."

"Where do you get these ideas from?"

The poet shrugged. The shrug intrigued the actor.

Next to them was an English novelist. She had been paying keen attention to their conversation. Her next novel was going to be about life and death.

The play they would be seeing was about Mahler's conversion from Judaism to Christianity. He had converted to get the job as senior conductor in Vienna. The performance was for a charity event. The photographer appeared and the invited guests gathered for the photographs that would help draw attention to the charity event. The conversation passed on to more pragmatic things.

The next time the poet saw the actor was at the charity event itself, which took place after the performance of the play. The production, a little bare, was enjoyed by the poet. The novelist walked out of the play before the interval.

Most of the guests did not enjoy the play as much as the poet did. His taste in these matters was relaxed. He appreciated the trouble people took to create something and never allowed himself to become snobbish. If he was amused, stimulated, and delighted a little, if there was some humor in the work, some profundity, he was generally contented. He felt that too much shouldn't be asked of living artists. Too much straining and they make life dull.

He spoke to several people at the party. He had a lively moment with a Jewish couple talking about their favorite play of the twentieth century, which was Arthur Miller's *The Crucible*.

"Why?" he asked the man.

The man shrugged. "Great metaphor," he said. "And you, what do you choose?"

"*The Cherry Orchard*," the poet replied.

"Why?"

"Its deceptive transparency."

"Is that all?"

"No."

"What else?"

"Its perfect poetic narrative and the mysterious parable at its heart."

"Good reasons," the woman said.

Not long afterward he met the elderly actor again. They exchanged greetings warmly.

"I might have a part for you in a play of mine," the poet said.

"You have a play?"

"It's been maturing in my cupboard for twenty years."

The elderly actor seemed surprised, and said: "Would you like to come and see my play?"

"Your play?" the poet said.

"One I'm directing."

"I'd be delighted."

"I'll give you a call to fix the ticket and arrange a date," the elderly actor said, before leaving.

A week passed. The actor called and arranged the ticket for a Wednesday. This was later canceled because it was press night. The actor said he found press nights stressful. A few days later the actor fixed the ticket for the following Wednesday. He suggested dinner afterward.

"Is it okay if I bring my partner?" the poet said.

"Absolutely."

On the day itself the actor and the poet were late, but the partner was early. It was a time when the world was uneasy with the war in Afghanistan. In response to the destruction of the Twin Towers, America was dropping bombs on Kabul. The world felt raw and dangerous, perched on the edge of a world war that could drag on indefinitely. People feared terrorist attacks on major Western cities would paralyze their lives. It was a strange time, the fire-birth of a new century.

It was in this nervous world atmosphere that they gathered at the Court Theatre bar. They had a drink and went up to see the play. It was a series of three monologues. It had only two characters. The experience was uncomfortable, but the play was not without some feeling. After the play they converged downstairs for another quick drink, and went to dinner at Como Lario.

Dinner was delightful. Their host, the elderly actor, was pleasant and charming. He was a good listener, a careful cultivator of his energies, and a Scot, as it turned out. He had been fortunate to find fame late in life, when his character was already formed and his mind unassailable. This made him comfortable to be with. He was a pragmatist who enjoyed a good laugh.

The two tables next to them were occupied by young stockbrokers who talked loudly and were brash in their jokes. The actor scowled at them during dinner.

At their table they talked about many things. They talked about their childhoods, about once-famous plays that were deserting the world like reproachful friends. They talked about shows they had liked or hated. They talked about directors who were in fashion, actors falling out of favor, and of the absence of courage in many new plays being written. But they didn't talk about mysteries.

"Tell me about your play."

The poet spoke briefly and shyly about the play he had written, and which he felt had a special role for the actor.

"When can I read it?"

"It needs a bit of work. Maybe in a month or two?"

"I'd love to read it whenever you are ready."

Dinner came to an end with cappuccino and teas. The actor paid the bill, left a generous tip, and gave the noisy young things at the next table his signature scowl. Then they went out into the chilly October night.

"Can I give you a lift?" he asked, hailing a taxi.

"Thank you, but we'll walk for a bit."

"Are you sure?"

"Yes. Thank you."

"It's no trouble."

"That's kind of you, but we'll be fine."

They said their goodbyes. The actor climbed into the taxi, and left.

They had declined the offer of a lift because they wanted to walk. They loved walking. The poet and his girlfriend, who was a painter, walked everywhere they could. They loved the conversations that walking yields.

It had rained, the sidewalks were wet, and a strong wind was blowing. The streets were quiet and the air was fresh. They wanted to walk for a while, and then catch a late bus home.

They went down a side street, talking about the play. They hadn't liked it much, but they really liked the actor. Events of the day filtered through their conversation, along with incidental shafts of philosophy and speculation. They came to a bus stop. They were far from their normal bus routes. They waited in the dark for a bus that might take them close to home. The streets were still and silent after the rain.

They were waiting patiently when a slick black car appeared, like an apparition, in front of them. It had slid out of nowhere, quietly, suddenly. It had glided into their space. A smooth, handsome young man was at the wheel. There was something sinister about him which they could not place. The front-seat window came down silently. The man at the wheel looked at them without speaking.

At that same moment, along the deserted street, a bouncer in a nightclub stepped out into the lighted doorway and became visible. He was thickset in a black suit and a white shirt. He turned and looked in their direction.

Then the young man spoke. "Sloane Street?" he said. He was European, German or Italian.

"I don't know where that is," the poet's girlfriend said.

"We're not from around here," said the poet.

"Sloane Street?" the man in the car asked again.

"Ask that chap," the poet said, pointing at the bouncer.

The sinister young man in the slick car did not look in the direction indicated. He lingered. He waited. He watched the two of them. He smiled in a curious way. There was something odd about the way he held his head, something unfathomable about the dark light in his eyes. He waited much longer than he needed to. It was as if he wanted something, or as if he were giving them a chance to want something from him.

Then the girlfriend stepped forward and said: "Try someone else."

That broke the spell. The car glided away as mysteriously as it had appeared. They didn't really see it go. It just disappeared, and they moved on to other thoughts. It was only later that it gained significance.

They stood there for some time in the car's wake. The sudden pointlessness of everything swept over them. They felt restless and a malaise crept into them.

"What are we waiting for?" the poet wondered aloud.

"Nothing," the painter said. "Let's walk."

"Yes."

"The air is good."

They walked to the square. It was almost empty. They had a choice of roads to take. They looked for bus stops. It was late now. Something had pulled them there. They stood in the square for a long time. They stood there, staring at the night, at the buildings, the empty taxis, waiting for nothing.

"Let's walk toward Knightsbridge," the poet said.

"Okay. It's that way," his girlfriend said, pointing down a street, which she later realized was Sloane Street.

"No, let's go down this street," the poet said, indicating the street just ahead of them. "That street looks uninteresting at this hour."

"Maybe this is not its hour."

"This one ahead looks more alive."

They crossed the road. It was a clear and fine night. The wind was warm. There was a perfect mood in the air.

Harmony dwelled between the poet and his girlfriend. She was happy. She loved the wandering mood they were in. It reminded her of an Italian holiday, roaming in a strange little town at night, with a sense of wonder and romance.

They came to a bus stop and found that one of the buses could take them in a homeward direction. They stood there a while. Walking was their original aim, but there they were again lingering at that bus stop. That was the poet's doing. He was just standing there, feeling and not knowing what he felt. He had a sense that there was something he should be aware of, something he should be seeing. He looked in the distance and saw a red double-decker bus far away, close to where they had been. He said nothing. This numinous feeling filled his being.

They were both silent. He gazed at the stars, at the night sky, not thinking.

Then she said: "C1."

The poet looked down. He had heard her say: "See one."

Then he saw the bus. It was a single-decker bus, with the legend *C1* on its destination panel. The poet said: "I see two."

"C1," she said again.

"I see two buses," the poet said, trying to be witty, but the original phrase he had heard still echoed in his mind.

The C1 bus stopped before them. Its door swung open. Its driver was African. A passenger stepped in, and the bus drove off.

The second bus the poet had seen stood at the same spot, far away, at a junction in Sloane Square. It stood there, red in the night, for a long time. They both stared. A gentle breeze blew their minds to other distractions. Suddenly the poet heard her words like a spell opening up the night.

"Look at that church!"

A little alarmed, the poet looked and saw the church. It was strange, out of place, beautiful. It belonged in some quaint Italian town. Something stumbled upon as you wandered at night in a strange city, senses open to wonder.

The church was just opposite the bus stop, at the end of a short street. Its modest elongated dome made an enchanting shape in the night sky.

"It's like something in a dream," she said.

The poet received the presence of the church without amazement, almost coolly.

"Something is missing from the church," he said simply.

"What's missing?"

"I don't know. But I feel the absence of something."

"What?"

The poet was silent. This absence that he felt made him unusually aware. He began looking where he shouldn't be looking. Then he saw it.

"I see one," he said.

"What?"

He directed with his gaze. Then she saw it too. There it

was in the middle of the street. It was as clear as an illumination. It was composed of the square shapes of manholes. Beautiful in form and perspective, a marvel of the golden mean, it was a perfect cross. It led the eye to the unusually situated church; and the church, by indirection, returned the eye to the perfection of the cross. The two things could only be seen from the bus stop.

"It's a secret sign," she said.

"Meant only for those inclined to see it."

"We don't really notice things, do we?"

"No, we don't. We look, but we see nothing."

"We notice nothing."

"Why do you think that is?"

"I don't know," she said. "Maybe we've drained away from the world the mystery with which it is made."

Staring at the conjunction of the church and the sign, they pondered many possibilities in silence. They had the sense of a secret world at work in our world. They had an intuition of many things besides, too incredible but perfectly possible. Notions that couldn't be shared except with the like-minded.

Then the bus, which had been unaccountably delayed at the red lights, glided into the bus stop. It was empty. The driver smiled at them. They got on, climbed upstairs, took seats at the large front windows, and gazed at the unseen world.

Tulips

First you go to an exhibition. You see a Hoover machine and shiny advertisements and a huge punani being made love to by the artist. You see vitrines and cartoon characters in superrealism. The gallery is big and has high ceilings and high white walls and staircases that are works of art.

It's not the exhibition you go there for, but the space. You are there to see the space and how it will harbor a cave and an open matchbox and the core of an apple on the floor. You don't remember if there were flowers in the exhibition.

It's getting dark and you can hear the trains grinding on the tracks as they run past overhead. The sound of the rhythm of trains punctuates the November night.

You are there with someone who is pregnant and the spirit of this child with a half smile follows you around. At the end of the exhibition the girl behind the till gives you a present of a book for the child not yet born but who somehow communicates her presence.

There were flowers on a ledge near the entrance but we didn't notice them when we came in. They weren't tulips.

On another day we had a filmed conversation in the gallery. Then we had dinner upstairs in the pharmacy, or was it the hospital? Everyone was healthy and the food was good. We talked about art.

There was a man sitting next to my friend's wife. He looked unmistakably Dutch. He had a pile of brochures. The conversation for the rest of dinner was about tulips.

The Dutchman was a tulip salesman. I expected him to have at least a passing resemblance to a tulip. I had a definite image of what a tulip looked like till I looked in the brochures. There were a thousand permutations. The tulip salesman sold hundreds of thousands of tulips every year. I didn't know there were that many on the planet. I saw tulips of all colors and sizes, but not all shapes. I didn't see a spherical tulip, nor a triangular one, nor a tulip that looked like a dog. There was talk of tulip soup and tulip burgers. There was no talk of the tulip crash.

Toward the end of dinner I was surprised to discover that the salesman had more than a passing resemblance to a blond tulip I saw in the brochure. I walked across the bridge after dinner and the word tulip kept repeating itself in my head. It was a very cold night and I paused in the middle of the bridge and stared down into the dark river of tulips. All the big houses with their lighted windows wove themselves into tulip buildings and the bus rode by on tulip wheels.

When I got home my girlfriend asked me what the evening was like.

"Lovely," I said.

"How was Gavin?"

"He was a tulip."

"Oh. How was Deborah?"

"She was a tulip too, with a gorgeous hat."

"Interesting. How was dinner?"

"Excellent."

"Really? What did you have?"

"Tulip soup."

"Extraordinary. What did it taste like?"

"It tasted like a poem I read one night when I was a kid."

The Lie

There was once a king obsessed by the search for truth. After many years of being unable to get any closer to it, he chose an opposite method. He sent his courtiers, his wizards, philosophers, magicians, and even his fool on an important mission.

They were to travel to all corners of the world and find out from every man, woman, or child what constituted the greatest lie in the lives of human beings. He hoped that by finding out the greatest lie he would, by deduction, arrive at the greatest truth. He was so determined on this mission that he dedicated extensive resources to its fulfillment.

For many years his emissaries traveled all the lands of the earth asking people what they considered the greatest lie. After a long absence they returned to him. To each one he posed his questions. Their answers surprised him.

The first to return was the court librarian. He had lost

a considerable amount of weight. The gifts he brought back with him were richly bound rare books from all over the world.

"I don't recognize you," said the king.

"Your Majesty, I am the court librarian. I have been gone these seven years."

"I'm sorry I didn't recognize you, but you are much changed."

"The journey has aged me. I have learned much. Time on a quest is different from time in the library."

"What have you found to be the greatest lie?"

"The greatest lie is that there is life after death."

"Why is this a lie?"

"We have not been able to prove it."

"What is the effect of this lie?"

"If there is no life after death then people can do whatever they want while they are alive. This breeds great audacity in evil deeds and a feeling that people can get away with anything. Those who believe there is no life after death are on the whole rather sad people. Life has no meaning for them. A life without meaning is a terrible thing, Your Majesty."

The king lavished fine gifts on the librarian. The librarian departed and resumed his office.

The next to return was his chief horseman. His hair was white. He too had aged.

"Who are you?"

"I am your chief horseman."

"You're much altered."

"The faster I traveled the less I discovered. I came to see that speed was a hindrance. So I traveled on foot. The things I learned humbled me. I am now resolved to sit still."

"Perhaps your return will restore you to your love of horses. What did you learn to be the greatest lie?"

"The greatest lie is that there is no life after death."

"Quite the opposite to what we heard before. Why is it a lie?"

"We have been able to prove there is life after death. I met a very young girl who remembered her family from her last life. They were hundreds of miles away. She led us to them and on the way told us things about this family that only children from that family could have known. There were many cases like this."

"I see," said the king. "What is the effect of this lie?"

"Those who felt there was life after death did not fear death. This made a difference to how they lived. They were happier people. It seems, Your Majesty, that what we feel about death is the quality that most determines the kind of life we lead."

The king sent him back to his stables with fine presents. The magician was the next to return. He was dressed in white. He had not aged at all. The king recognized him immediately.

"You are my magician. Welcome back from your quest."

"Thank you, Your Majesty. I bring gifts from the Far East, lapis lazuli and gold. I have been gone seven years and have seen many wonders and evils. I have heard more lies than a man can withstand."

"You look exactly the same, but you seem different."

"The quest has altered me. I have seen so many kinds of magic that I am now determined to live a simple life without magic. Life seems to me now the greatest magic of all."

"We value the magic you brought to our court. Maybe your return will cure you of your renunciation. What is the greatest lie that you found on your journeys?"

"The greatest lie I found was that people have been led to believe that when they grow up they will be happy."

"And is this not true?"

"No, Your Majesty. It seems people grow sadder as they grow older. They look back on the period of their childhood as a paradise they have lost."

"What is the effect of this lie?"

"Disappointment."

"Thank you, Court Magician. Our vizier will reward you for the quest you have undertaken. We hope that you return to your magic books renewed."

"Simplicity is my new magic, Your Majesty."

The king nodded, a little sadly. The magician departed.

And so they returned, in a steady stream. One courtier said the great lie consisted in being told in childhood that people were good and that life was fair. The philosopher said that the great lie was that time was real.

"Is time not real?" said the king.

"It seems time is unreal, an illusion."

"Does time not pass? Have you not been away for seven years?"

"Time passes differently for different people," said the court philosopher. "For a lover waiting to see his beloved time is slow. To someone late for an appointment time is fast. People find time puzzling, Your Majesty. For an old man the memory of life is shorter than a day, and to a child the sense of the future is longer than eternity."

The philosopher departed, with gifts. Then it was announced that the fool had returned from his travels. Of all his emissaries the king was particularly interested in the findings of his fool.

"So, my fool, you have returned at last."

"Your Majesty, I am not sure I have returned at last. I have returned at fifth."

"But you have returned?"

"I can still turn, when it is my turn to do so."

"What will you turn from?"

"I could turn from myself, but heaven knows what I will turn into. Besides, my coat will not let me."

"Why will your coat not let you, Fool?"

"Because I am not a turncoat."

"I see that seven years away has not made you less a fool."

"Your Majesty, I see that the years here have not made you any less a king."

"Why should they?"

"If one does one thing too long one ends up doing its opposite."

"How so?"

"Time turns all things around."

"How is this possible?"

"Because the world goes round."

"Have you seen it go round?"

"I have become round since I have been away. That's how I know it goes round."

"Enough of this banter," said the king. "Tell us your findings."

"The great lie, Your Majesty, is that your power is real."

"What do you mean by that?" roared the king.

Unperturbed, the fool went on: "Your power is unreal. It is made of air. It consists of what we have conferred on you. You are our creation, our fiction. We have taken our power and given it to you. Then we forgot that you were made by us."

"Is this what you have brought back to me?"

"No."

"There is more?"

"There is more."

"What is it?"

"The real lie, Your Majesty, is that we individuals have

no power. We keep looking for power elsewhere. But we are powerful. On my travels I met a wise man who told me a great secret."

"What is the secret?" the king asked, leaning forward.

"The secret is that the least is the most, and the most is the least."

"What does that mean?"

"Your Majesty, I am only a fool. I cannot do your thinking for you."

The king glared at his fool. At a signal the soldiers seized him.

"Behead him for his insolence!"

As he was being dragged away, the fool shouted: "If I am beheaded, Your Majesty, the joke will be on you."

"Stop!" said the king. "Bring him back!"

The soldiers brought back the fool.

"What joke?"

"There will be two jokes."

"What are they?"

"The first is that the king killed his fool because his fool told him that he was a king."

"And the second?"

"That the king asked for the greatest lie but couldn't handle the truth."

The king contemplated the fool for a while. Then the vizier came and whispered something in the king's ear.

"We will spare him for now," the king said.

The fool bowed. "Your wisdom surpasses your power," he said.

The king dismissed him, and awaited the other emissaries. The next day a child was brought to him.

"I know what the greatest lie is," said the child.

"What is it?"

"The greatest lie is that when people die they are gone forever."

"Why is this a lie?"

"Because three days after my mother died I saw her standing over my bed. She told me that all would be well."

"But were you not dreaming?" the king asked.

"That's what everyone says. But I was wide awake. Anyway, I saw her again."

"Where?"

"Three days later, in the marketplace."

"What is the lie?"

"That the dead are dead."

The king pondered this. He gave the child a small gift. He awaited others. A blind man was brought before him.

"The greatest lie, Your Majesty, is that the blind do not see."

"Is this true?"

"At first it was true of me. But one day I discovered I could see with eyes I didn't know I had. But I see in a strange light, as if everything were lit from within."

"What is the lie?" asked the king.

"It is twofold," the blind man said. "The first is that the blind cannot see. The second is that those who have sight can see. Maybe the latter is the greatest lie."

The blind man left, without any help, tapping his stick on the palace floor.

The king was struck by the blind man, but he awaited other messengers.

A few days later a woman was brought before the throne. She began wailing.

"Love is the greatest lie!"

"How so?" asked the king.

"I sought love and found nothing but ashes. Love has brought me more misery than anything else on earth. I have been abandoned, betrayed, deceived, and used. The poets sing too much about love, religion preaches it, but love as I have seen it is a name for something else."

"What can this be?"

"Lovers deceive themselves. They project onto one another, and see someone who is not there. When they eventually see the real person, they love no more. Love is a screen, it is a mirror, it is a blindness, it is a lie."

The king was perturbed by this, and sent the wailing woman away with gifts.

Then an old woman was brought before him. With the air of deep forests, with the rasping voice of an aged eagle, she said: "Of all the lies the greatest lie is truth."

The king was taken aback by this remark. "How can truth be the greatest lie?" he asked.

"Truth takes a thousand forms," said the old woman. "The truth of the fly is not the truth of the spider. The truth of your lowest servant is not that of the king. The truth of a man dying of a sword thrust is not the truth of the warrior plunging in the sword. The truth of fire is not that of ice. There is the truth of suffering and that of happiness, the truth of love and that of hate. The truth of death is not that of life. The skeleton speaks a different truth from the woman in the heat of lovemaking. Of all the things that have caused war and the greatest suffering, it is truth that is most responsible for them all. Every war is a war over truth. All sides dispute it. We all believe we have our truth. But no one has seen the truth. Some say God is truth, but none have seen God. Some say Love is truth, but none have seen Love. Truth is a mirage that has led man astray in the deserts of time."

With this the old woman left, and the king was much diminished.

He had grown old awaiting his messengers. He had grown weary listening to the innumerable forms of the greatest lie brought to him over the years. Not a day passed in which he wasn't presented with a version of the great lie. The king believed he had heard them all. He had heard all the lies about being human. He had heard about the lies that people tell themselves. Listening to all the lies had slowly drained him of life. All illusions fled from his heart. His spirit grew dry. There seemed nothing left of any splendor in the world.

The king had heard the lie in all its infinite forms. He had heard political lies, intellectual lies, and spiritual lies. Nothing that we see is as it seems: sight is a lie. Nothing that we hear is as it sounds: hearing is a lie. The senses deceive. Memory falsifies. Time is an illusion. Life is unreal. Death is unknowable. Even power succumbs to the law that what is given can be taken away.

It is possible that all these years he had not been a king, but an old man listening to the whisperings of fables in the wind.

The king grew old and found one day that he was at the golden door of death. With a sigh he passed into the night. Then he heard the voice of an angel whisper to him: "All your life you sought truth. Then you sought the lie. Everything you were told was the truth and a lie. Did you learn anything?"

The king said: "I learned everything and nothing. I listened to the tales of travelers."

The angel said: "Then your whole life was a lie."

"In which case," said the king, "I am on the verge of truth."

That was when the king found that he too was a messenger of a greater king, who awaited the distillation of his research.

Boko Haram (2)

They sent us out into the forests of the North. We'd never been there before. We had heard things. They didn't bear thinking about, the things we had heard.

They sent us out with six bullets each. Most of our guns were old. Our boots were old and patched. We couldn't waste a single bullet and we didn't know how long the engagement would last. We didn't know who we were fighting. We'd only heard things.

Our uniforms had holes in them. No one knows what happened to all the money allocated for our uniforms and guns and bullets and good boots. They sent us out with nothing.

We went into the forest and every sound made us jump. We didn't even have good trucks. It was so bad sometimes only the weed consoled us. We went into the forest and nothing happened for a long time.

We went in deep. Our officer didn't know where we were. It was awfully quiet in the forest. Six bullets each we had, and that was it.

We came to a place where we saw a man hanging. He was one of us. Hanging from a tree. His tongue cut out and his mouth black and many of us sick seeing it.

That was when they jumped out. They were wild and had machine guns and their eyes were red and they seemed happy to find us. They had been waiting. It didn't take long for us to fire our six bullets.

Then they came at us all at once, firing their rounds without stop, making faces.

They were having quite a time of it.

We the army, the nation's army, turned around and dropped our empty guns and ran.

You were lucky if you got out of there alive.

The Master's Mirror

I first heard about the mirror at a meeting of Rosicrucians in Hampstead. I had been invited to the meeting by a doctor I met at a party. He was a man of trim appearance, hawklike eyes, and exact manners. He gave the impression of precision in all things.

The doctor and I fell into a conversation about parallel streams of history. We discovered that we shared an interest in alternative explanations for many mysterious historical events. I think I made a casual reference to the Rosicrucians and their legendary reality.

"There are many groups around today calling themselves by that name," he said.

"But which is the real one?"

"What is the real truth?"

"About what?"

"Exactly. Truth is both singular and multiple. There

are as many Rosicrucians as there are paths to the ultimate truth."

While I brooded on this aphorism, he said: "Why don't you come to our next meeting?"

"Our?"

"Yes. It should interest you."

As he spoke I experienced that frisson one feels when approaching the solving of some abiding mystery.

"Do you mean . . ."

"Speak no more of it in public," he said.

Then he scribbled down an address on a little pad and brought the conversation to a close with a mysterious smile. He started to move away, but came back to give me exact instructions.

"You are to do exactly as I told you, or you will not be admitted," he said.

I thanked him for his trust. He was inviting a stranger to a meeting that must require careful selection. I felt honored. Near us a group of people were talking about the forth-coming elections.

One moment the doctor was nodding at me, and the next he was gone. The manner of his disappearance was in keeping with the fantastical things I had heard about Rosicrucians.

The meeting was due to take place on a Saturday, in the early afternoon. I took the Underground. In Hampstead it was a splendid September day. There was fine sunlight on the beech trees. With a sense of its urban mystery, I went down Hampstead Hill, past the big old silent houses. Oleanders and heliotropes were in bloom along the quiet streets.

The house was at the bottom of the hill. It was white and had a tiled ocher roof and vines on its walls. It seemed more than a hundred years old.

The doorbell gave no evidence of working. Only when I began to explore other means of gaining the attention of those inside did the door open suddenly. Its hinges needed oiling. I glimpsed doors behind doors, a warren of chambers within.

A bearded and severe-looking man, with a faint Aleister Crowley air, looked at me quizzically. When I said nothing, he began to shut the door. I felt invisible.

"I am expected," I said.

"We are all expected somewhere," he said blithely.

"I am expected here."

"Expectations are dangerous."

The remark silenced me a moment.

"By whom?"

"What?"

"Who is expecting you?"

"Someone who gave me an invitation. A doctor."

"Someone presumably with a name?"

"He didn't give me his name."

"What form did it take, if I may be so bold as to ask?"

"Did what?"

"The invitation."

"Words."

"Not good enough," he said, after subjecting me to a long stare.

I was thrown by this. The invitation, as I recall, had been simple. I was to be at a certain place, at a certain time. I was to ring the doorbell. Then I was to say I was expected. That was all.

The Crowley man stared at me till I began to doubt my own reality. He waited patiently without appearing to be waiting for anything. I racked my memory. What had I forgotten? Then I remembered the doctor had said something about bringing a rose. I had not heard it at the time. I heard it afterward.

I had brought the rose, not thinking for a moment that anyone would expect me to produce it before admitting me to the meeting. Delicately I took out the slightly crushed rose from my inner coat pocket and tentatively presented it to the guardian. He stood up straight and brightened.

"It seems you are expected here," he said, and led me into the precincts of the order.

2

The guardian led me into a room from another century,

teeming with musty tomes. An engraving of Christian Rosenkreutz hung on the wall. A solitary skull adorned an alcove. Magical implements, somewhat rusted, were ranged along the mantelpiece. I saw a sword with a black hilt, a tapering wand, a black hat, and a pair of calipers on a side table. They had an air of casual enchantment. Ancient books of astrology and the kabbalah, books by Jacob Boehme and Paracelsus, made their presence felt from the bookshelves.

Sitting in a circle, on household chairs, were thirteen brethren. The man who had invited me sat on a royal high chair, at the head of the gathering. Before him was a table of solid mahogany. On it were an old heavy leather-bound bible, an ancient copy of the *Fama Fraternitatis*, and an astrolabe.

He didn't seem to recognize me. I barely recognized him. He was enveloped in a black cloak with a gold clasp. Jewels of his authority hung from his neck. I made out a golden globe surmounted by a cross. He had an aura of medieval authority and his gestures were measured and theatrical. He was the magus of that branch of the order.

I was briefly introduced to the others. They regarded me from a great distance. In that atmosphere I experienced two contradictory feelings. I felt I was embarked on a time travel, and at the same time I felt I was beneath a murky sea.

The lecture was about a mirror first acquired by Frederick Hockley, an occultist of the nineteenth century. He was born in Lambeth, London. His life abounded with the ambiguities that history dislikes. Educated in Hoxton, he later worked for an occult bookseller in Covent Garden. This was perhaps responsible for his subsequent fascination with the art of scrying.

Then in 1884, after thirty years of practicing the art, Hockley consecrated a large mirror. He dedicated it to what he professed was his spirit guide, known only by the initials C.A. The purpose of this consecration was to be inspired and to receive answers to a variety of metaphysical questions about the mysteries of existence. He devoted Tuesdays to this arcane activity.

How the mirror acquired its reputation remains difficult to explain. It is believed that Hockley and his friends had many visions in the mirror. It made its way into the hands of Madame Blavatsky. Then it came into the possession of the high council of the order.

There were rumors that the source of the mirror's visions owed less to the world of spirits and more to tinctures of laudanum and opium much in use in Victorian times for medicinal purposes. There were other rumors that the mirror had actually been given to Hockley by Madame Blavatsky, about whom he had been rude in his private correspondences.

An avid collector of books, with over two thousand volumes on the shelves of his accommodation, Hockley died in 1885 of what the doctors called "natural decay" and "exhaustion." The irony is that at the end he suffered from poor eyesight.

But the facts of Hockley's life do not begin to account for the mystery of the mirror.

At this point the magus paused. He looked around at the circle of bearded occultists and hermeticists.

"The fact is that Hockley's mirror has a frightening legend," he said, wiping his face with a cambric handkerchief. "It has been locked up in a vault by the high council for over a hundred years. It has only been brought out twice. This is the third time."

The magus seemed nervous. He kept glancing at the only woman in the circle. She was in her early sixties, pleasant looking and dressed with good taste. She kept a steady eye on the magus as if to strengthen him while his nerves faltered.

"The mirror of which I speak has an abominable reputation. Apparently one must gaze into it only after having undergone the utmost preparation."

He sipped from a glass of water on the table before him.

"It is said that if one looks into the mirror one might not see oneself reflected. And if this happens . . ."

He paused again.

"If this happens the person might go mad. Or die soon afterward."

He made a longer pause. Then he brought out a fob-watch from his waistcoat pocket, and stared at it a long time, apparently lost in thought.

After a full minute, he snapped shut the fob-watch, and gazed at us as if seeing us for the first time.

"There have already been two tragic incidents. The first man who looked into the mirror, in the early years of the twentieth century, went mad two days later."

He looked at each one of us. The expression on his face was slightly strained.

"Then the assisting magus of the order, thirty years ago, at a special convention, looked into the mirror. The next day he died in mysterious circumstances. The coroner's report was inconclusive. It seems his heart had simply, suddenly, stopped."

He paused again. This time he appeared to be staring at me. It was a stare so intense that I came out in a sweat. I brought out a handkerchief to dry my face, but when I leaned forward I realized he was not staring at me but into emptiness.

"You may wonder why I am telling you these facts. For many years now there has been much debate among senior members of the council about the efficacy of the mirror. Things gain their reputation from fear, from superstition, and from a faulty connection between significant events. We are rationalists. We live in the age of science. It is time to test the theory of the mirror."

A gasp was heard from the back of the room. Several

faces turned toward me. I assured them that the sound had come from elsewhere.

"My plan is twofold. First, to present my lecture. And then, at a certain hour, under the strictest precautions taken by my wife and myself, to gaze into Hockley's mirror."

We stared at him dimly.

"This time next week we will know the results. Either I shall participate in the ancient art of scrying, and communicate with C.A., Hockley's spirit guide, or my name will be linked to the monstrous reputation of Hockley's mirror forever."

He took off his glasses, gave them an expert polishing, put them back on, and parsed our faces.

"Like most of you I have a profound interest in the mysteries. But I am also a man of science. And scientists test the limits of the known."

The magus broke off his speech and a hearty applause followed. The applause was out of keeping with the austere mood of the gathering. Then with a final ritual the meeting was brought to a close.

In the outer chamber there were tea and cakes. With cups of tea and cakes on small round plates, we chatted about infamous mirrors through the ages. I found myself talking to the magus's wife.

"The lecture was fascinating," I said, "but are you not concerned about the risk your husband is taking?"

"It's not much of a risk," she said, to my surprise.

"Oh, why not?"

"Because I have looked into the mirror myself."

I reared backward with involuntary horror.

"I took the greatest precautions," she said, smiling at the effect her words had on me.

"Did you? What did you do?"

"I said the prescribed prayers, surrounded myself with red candles, and invoked the appropriate assistance. There are things you can do. But the preparation must be rigorous."

"When was this?" I was wondering about the time it might take for the dreaded effect.

She read my thoughts. "I saw myself in the mirror," she said.

"Oh."

But her next remark drained the blood from my face. "There was something strange about it."

"What?"

"I heard a faint voice in its depths. Then I noticed that the face in the mirror wasn't mine. It was someone who looked like me. Someone who was trying on my face, as it were."

I didn't quite know what to say.

"I knew it wasn't me. The face in the mirror was a mask. I could see it in the eyes. They were not my eyes. That's when I heard the voice."

"What did it say?" I asked.

"The voice said: 'Tell your husb—'"

At that moment the magus appeared among us. "Time to go now," he said, taking her by the hand.

I was surprised that he still didn't recognize me. He seemed preoccupied. I congratulated him on his talk. With a blank gaze, he murmured something about inaccuracies.

"Oh, it's you," he said brightly. "I am glad you could come."

We made small talk. Then, abruptly, he said he must be going. Seizing his wife by the hand, he went out of the door, waving as he left.

Thirty minutes later, I was climbing Hampstead Hill. I lingered in a few bookshops. I was unable to shake the impression the talk made on me. That night I had a nightmare in which Hockley came out of the mirror and asked me to lend him my face. He was tearing off my face when I woke up.

3

The next Saturday I made my way back to the secret address in Hampstead. I rang the bell twice. The third time the door opened, as if on cue. Upon receipt of a fresh rose from me, I was led to the inner circle.

There was an atmosphere of gloom. No one said anything to me. The magus was not at the high council table. His wife was also absent. There was a black rose in the magus's seat.

We were led through a prayer in Latin. Then we brooded

in silence. After an hour of the funereal atmosphere, the deputy magus stood up and made an enigmatic speech. He spoke in numbers.

"Our magus," he said, "has left nine and joined with ten. He was the sublime four. Sometimes we gaze into twelve and lose the unity of one. We fragment into two, unable to be reconciled by seven. Then we are delivered into the mud of five."

His finely shaven head seemed a miniature of the Easter Island statues. He had hooded eyes and an ascetic mouth. I didn't recognize him from the last meeting. He paused and gazed at us nearsightedly.

"The world is perceived by our mind. When we stare into the mirror of the world, it is we who stare back—as strangers."

He joined his palms together. A small gold Egyptian symbol hung around his neck, resting on his black tunic. He had been standing to the side of the magus's table. Then he took a short step, till he was in front of it. His voice rose slightly.

"I have consulted with the high council. They have voted unanimously that the mirror of Hockley will be returned to the vault, never to be unveiled again. Our magus will have the distinction of being the last human being ever to have looked into the master's mirror."

The short oration seemed to leave him gasping for air. He struggled with a thought he wanted to impart. He appeared to decide against it. Then shaking his head, he smiled.

"Our magus left behind a short statement. It can only be shared with senior officers of the order. After this meeting, in proper ceremonial fashion, the message will be delivered. For now, brethren, remember that the quintessence of five will rise out of the elixir of three. Combining with the resonance of seven, it will ascend to the mystery of twenty-two. Then mounting the branching paths of light, it will reunite us again, in the effulgence of one, with our ever-present master."

He brought his speech to a close, and slid out of a door I had not noticed before. The door was the bookshelf. When it shut behind him, the only book that seemed disturbed was by Cornelius Agrippa.

No tea or cakes were served afterward. Those of us who were visitors found ourselves on the gravel of the forecourt, near the fading wisteria, blinking in the surprise of sunlight, like owls.

Without a word, we went our different ways into the branching streets of Hampstead.

4

One beautiful Sunday, six months later, I was wandering about on Hampstead Heath with a friend. She was a painter and like me was given to metaphysical speculation. I had confided to her the unlikely story of the mirror.

We stood on the brow of the hill. The sweep of the sky made us thoughtful. Far off could be seen the Houses of Parliament. Children were rolling down the hill.

As we gazed at the city, my friend said: "The reality of the world is more incredible than we are taught."

Then she wandered off to find motifs for the day's painting.

I stood staring at the magnificence of the world. After a while I made my way down the hill and sat on a bench by the lake. I watched the changing colors of the sky on the face of the water.

The bench was empty when I sat down. I hadn't been there long when someone sat on the bench next to me. The intrusion irritated me, but after a moment I suddenly experienced a sense of peace.

I didn't look to see who it was, but went on staring at the surface of the lake, and made the not surprising discovery that the lake was also a mirror. Gazing at its reflections, lost in a serene mood, I was transported.

"All things incline to our liberation, if we know how to use them," said a voice from the lake, jolting me back to the present.

The air about me changed. There was no one around. The man who sat next to me was gone.

The shadow of a heron flew low over the gray-blue waters.

The Standeruppers

For some time we had seen them trying to crouch. We had seen them reaching for something in the air that was not there.

From the sky a god was wetting the earth with the vigor of their water. Another god was growling. The earth was answering. We were dancing in the water of the gods.

It was a good day. We had followed the beast across the grass. We had followed it morning and night. Someone had brought an image of the beast in the chants they made and we saw the beasts in our heads as if they were right there. We ran with our four legs when we chased the beasts across the grass. We had sharp stones to stab them with. We dreamed of them all night in the cave.

When blackness comes we wait to see what the god of night will do with our sleep. Then we go to the place where we can do anything. There are many other beings there that we do not know. We watch them all night. When the light-god returns, the other place goes with our getting up.

2

The best among us were the crouchers. We crouched in the round light of the light-god. Those on four legs moved fast but low. The tall grass moved when they moved but you could not see them.

We ran across the dust. I saw one moving on three legs. We thought it odd. We growled at him later as we tore the flesh of the beast with our teeth. He growled back with an odd face. As if he knew something. We thought of killing him.

So fast it all changed. No one knows how. Many times the blackness came. The round white in the sky moved over the grass. Many things we saw on the other side of the dark where the shadow people live.

3

Then someone showed us something not there before in the cave. We saw the beasts on the cave walls. We tried to kill them but they would not die. Much redness came from us in that battle with the wall. Then we saw one laughing. Watching us and laughing as we fought beasts on the cave wall.

We thought we were on the other side of the dark where we went when we closed our eyes. But the beast was there on that wall. The other one was laughing as our sticks broke against the beasts that would not move on the wall. They were not beasts you could touch or eat. Made of rock. They made us hungry.

When the light-god came back and we could see, we went to find the beasts in the grass. We knew how to fight them now that they were made of stone.

4

The one who laughed did not come with us. Something was strange about him. We crouchers had to look up at him, with the light-god in our eyes. As we went we thought of killing him. But his laughter filled us with fear.

The beast was easier to kill now that we had fought it on the wall. We feared it less.

So many noises we made. With our sharp stones we waited. When it ran at us we crouchers were ready. We jumped on its back.

But one who was not crouching found a way to hold its neck. Then its blood wet the earth. With our voices raised, we bore it home.

5

The one who laughed looked strange when we got back. He was as if risen. He began it all. The stretching, the reaching. Afterward the crouchers grew fewer. At first we wanted to kill those that did not crouch anymore, those that on two legs balanced.

Hard to be like them.

It took me many darknesses to walk with three feet, to stand on two legs.

Hair filled my face.

Those who did not crouch, who stood up, became leaders of the cave. One of them put the beasts on the cave walls in secret. He had the power of the gods. A woman worked with him. Both their eyes were dark.

6

They were the first standeruppers. We did not know what to do with them. But because of them it was easier to have meat between our teeth and grass under our heads.

Changing too fast. With the beasts and the cave walls and not crouching anymore, changing too fast.

I liked it best when the light-god rose over the grass.

Alternative Realities Are True

How wonderful that we have met with a paradox.
Now we have some hope of making progress.

NIELS BOHR

He woke one morning into a strange universe. Everything in his one-bedroom flat in Kensal Rise was exactly the same, but everything was also subtly different. He was not sure how.

There was a message for him on the answering machine which he listened to with the irritation the acute heat brought him. He hadn't been able to sleep. He'd been puzzling over his latest case. With each new piece of information he was finding it more troubling.

The message was from the office, delivered in a verbal encryption which he simultaneously deciphered. The dead man had been seen in the café at the canal. He looked through the crack in his curtains. It was nearly dawn. In his garden the blackbirds whistled their morning chorus. Usually, when he heard them he knew that sleep was over for him. This morning, there was something different about their tone.

Detective Draper got out of bed and slipped on his dressing gown and went to his study to review the case. On the face of it, the case was simple.

There had been a murder near him in Kensal Rise, but the body of the victim had not been found. There was no actual proof of murder, but there was knowledge of it. A young overwrought Muslim woman in a blue headdress who gave her name as Ana had come into the local police station. She had broken down and said a man she knew had been murdered. She gave his name. When asked how she knew he had been murdered, her eyes widened and she threw up her hands. She *knew*, she said. Who was the murdered man, who was he to her? she was asked.

But she would not say. Who was the killer? she was asked. At this she panicked and fled from the station. A few inquiries led them to her address and a watch was placed on the building.

A man by the name of Barrett, the assistant of a famous artist, went missing that same day. He had been known to frequent the woman's flat. This was a month ago. Barrett had still not been found.

Detective Draper, who believed more than anything

that intuition was superior to intellectual deduction, opposing himself to the theatrical methods of Sherlock Holmes, which had so captivated the police force, Scotland Yard, and the general public, knew that he was dealing with a case that amounted to more than the appearance of the facts. He believed that it was indeed essential to study a case thoroughly, to acquaint oneself with the locale of the crime, to handle the items of the principal players, in short to furnish the senses and instinct with all the available data and living facts possible, and then, like a fisherman who must commit himself to the sea, he must leave all those facts behind and trust to the mysterious dictates of intuition.

He had developed the faculty of intuition as a young man when he trained himself to be able to tell on which side a coin would fall, just by following the clearest whisper in his head. By slow degrees, applying this method to phone calls, knocks on doors, letters that he had received, guessing their contents and who sent them before opening them for verification, he had come to develop this mysterious faculty to a formidable degree.

Detective Draper never spoke about this to anybody, knowing full well that he would be a laughingstock if he did. He masked his secret technique behind a tremendous amount of paperwork and planning and detailed analyses. To all accounts, from the outside, he was an eminently practical detective, who did his research, and left nothing to chance. In truth he believed in the fertility of chance itself, which he did not regard as chance at all. He believed that all things in the universe were linked and that every fact was related to every other. From his armchair he solved his cases by indirection. He was the best in the force, his reputation unmatched.

That morning in his study, he went over the case methodically. He realized that there was something wrong with the facts of the case, some slight alteration of the world. For example, as soon as they put a watch on the Muslim woman's house certain other facts of the case shifted.

This was puzzling. The watch reported that, through the window, he had seen Ana's neighbor—a man named Jorg—cutting up a large chicken. The moment he noticed the chicken being cut up the lights in Ana's room had come on. Here was where it became baffling. The watch swore that he saw Jorg both cutting up the chicken and going into Ana's room at the same time. The watch was a sober man of unimpeachable reputation.

There were several other curious anomalies. Another, taken at random, was that when Jorg was seen cutting up the large chicken in his room, the reported victim of the murder was seen by witnesses in a café on the canal a few miles down the road. Those who saw him said that he looked well, if a bit anxious, and that he was reading a book at the time. Most of the witnesses could not recall the title of the book. Detective Draper did not think this at all unusual. Most people, he found, did not notice what was right under their noses. The inattentiveness of people was a constant source of amusement to him. He had come to rely on their failure to notice things. His best deductions came from working around the bends of this failure.

Questioning one of the witnesses he was able, through indirection, to work out the title of the book. To any other detective such a detail as the title of a book a victim was reading would be insignificant. But to Detective Draper nothing in the universe was insignificant. The witness remembered that in fact the victim was reading a cat.

"What do you mean he was reading a cat?"

"He was reading a cat."

"Did he have an actual cat in his hand?"

"Both hands."

"What color was the cat?"

"It did not have a color."

"Did it have a name?"

The last question had come to Detective Draper purely by intuition. It had simply dropped into his mind like that. But behind the intuition, hovering like the ghost of knowledge, was the understanding that some people see words as real things and that they are incapable of the abstract faculty of reading, transferring everything they read that has an image straightaway into its physical equivalent. This was one of those anomalous facts that the detective stored away in his mind.

"Yes, it did have a name."

"What was it?"

"It was a very strange name."

"Before you tell me what it was, tell me how you knew."

"It's strange, but I just did. I looked at the cat he was reading and its name popped into my head just like that."

"There is no need to tell me the name of the cat," the detective said, nonchalantly.

"Why not?"

"I know it already. But thank you."

The detective rose to signify the end of the interview, leaving the witness quite baffled. Detective Draper, absent-minded the moment he was consumed by a clue, called several bookshops. In a short time he found out what he wanted. A copy of the book had been purchased that day, quite early in the morning, from Any Amount of Books on Charing Cross Road. It was the only copy of the book purchased that morning. A check confirmed that the book had been bought by Jorg, as the detective had suspected. Another call to the local police station confirmed something else: that the victim had not been seen since. As it stood, there were two sightings. One was of the suspected killer in two places at the same time. The other was of the victim, after he had gone missing and was presumed dead.

For the rest of that day, contradictory reports kept pouring in. A warrant for the arrest of Jorg led to his detention. The large chicken he had been seen cutting up was brought in as evidence. But that same evening Jorg, who was in police custody, was seen in Ana's room. He was shouting at her and at one point called her a whore.

"I have killed that lover of yours and there's nothing anyone can do about it."

"What have you done to him?" she cried.

"I have hidden him where no one will ever be able to find him."

She was heard wailing, and Jorg was seen departing from the room. The watch was unable to do anything because he had conclusive proof that the murder suspect was in police custody. He had no legal right to arrest the same person twice.

Detective Draper considered the arrest of Jorg to have been an act of sublime stupidity by the local police.

The detective dropped in at the local station. The sergeant on duty, a thickset man, was reading Maigret. His name was Pillock and he had a reputation for brusqueness.

"The way I see it, Detective," he said, "is that we know a crime has been committed. But we have no evidence. We suspect it's a murder, but there is no body. And he could be a potential terrorist. We have to keep him locked up for the public good."

The detective contemplated Sergeant Pillock. There was no use arguing with him. Explanation was equally futile. He would have to add the heavy-footedness of the sergeant into the equation.

"But you do see that the problem multiplies?"

"I see that it simplifies."

"Any new evidence?"

"Only CCTV footage on a bus."

"What number?"

"Six. Is that significant?"

"Everything is significant. What did the footage yield?"

"Something puzzling."

"What?"

"The suspect made several trips in one direction with black plastic bags. He appeared to be moving house. We never saw him get off."

"Anything else?"

"Yes, but it doesn't make sense."

"Tell me."

"It stretches credibility."

"Let's have it."

"On one of the cameras we caught an image of the bus just as it exploded."

"Did it explode?"

"That's just it. It didn't. We believe the CCTV system has been hacked and false footage has been planted there."

"Unless there is an equally radical solution. But I fear we may be too late. We have to act fast."

"What shall we do?"

The detective did a rapid calculation. He felt himself encircled by time.

The first thing he did was order that the watch be pulled off Ana's house. Then he suggested that the suspect be released and not followed.

"Not followed?"

"No."

"But he must be followed."

"It will only make things worse."

"How?"

"We are being invaded by one of many possible futures."

"What was that?"

"Nothing. Forget it."

"Are you on something?"

"No, I'm sober as a surgeon on duty."

"Then you need to fill me in."

Detective Draper knew he could not explain the intuition that was filtering through to him. Wearily, he sought the most innocuous expression of it. He softened his voice as he spoke.

"Everything we do influences what the suspect does. We are multiplying the problem. Before, there was one murderer, now there are three."

"Three? Which three?"

"Free," the detective corrected himself. "I meant he should be free."

2

Detective Draper knew there were only two ways to resolve

the case. One was to prevent the murder, the other was to uncover it. All the evidence suggested it was too late to prevent the murder. It had happened. That past had now been lost. If the victim had been apprehended when he was seen reading the cat, things might have been different. That moment was gone. It was lost because no one noticed that the past lurks in the present. Not just past events, but the past as present.

Detective Draper liked to walk after he had been immersed in facts too long. When he had spent all day reading documents, studying evidence, listening to witnesses, when he was saturated with too much information, he would walk in a zigzag path through side streets to his home. Anyone seeing him would think he was wandering aimlessly. But his walks always followed the pattern of his thoughts. He had always known that the indirect route led more quickly to his destination. The direct routes were often bogged down in interruptions, conversations, and crowded streets.

That evening, after a long spell at the station, he left late.

His thoughts had gone off the map of indirection. He had taken so many side streets that he did not recognize where he was. He didn't mind. His best intuitions came while waking and while walking. In an odd way he seemed to be doing both now. He seemed to be waking from the sleep of his thoughts. Where was he? He looked around.

He had gone off the main road that led to his flat in Kensal Rise.

The street where he now stood looked decidedly strange. He searched for the street name, and found that he did not even recognize that. He walked on till he came to a barbershop. There were no customers. When he went in, he startled the barber who was reading a newspaper.

"Can you please tell me where I am?"

The barber stared at him with his mouth half open.

"Is anything wrong?"

"You came in here about five minutes ago," the barber said. "And you asked the very same question."

Detective Draper looked at the round clock on the wall with its Roman numerals. It was 6:35 p.m.

"So I did, so I did," Detective Draper murmured, and he hurried out.

He went back the way he had come. A glance told him that the barber had come out of his shop and was watching him. He walked faster, aware that the faster he walked the faster walked all the events connected to him. If he sped up, things would speed up too. The web of connected events responded to his every deed. Suddenly in his mind he could see the lines that linked him to the victim and the murderer and the woman. Except that these lines had multiplied in ways he could only guess at. He was walking aimlessly now, following the vectors of his thought. He conjectured that if he had arrived at this strange place by getting lost, then only by getting lost again could he return to a familiar world.

He was thinking fast and walking fast, as if something unknown were stalking him. The linking lines moved faster in his mind. Then he suddenly stopped. In the middle of all that wandering, a clear thought, distilled and pristine, dropped into his mind. Why hadn't he thought of it before?

There was now only one way to solve the murder. The past was closed to him. There was only one path left. He had to arrive at a future place before the murderer did. He had to outwit him in all the vectors of time. At this point the murderer had a time advantage over him. He had to overturn that advantage. He had to anticipate the murderer in the future.

He walked home much more slowly. He noticed the council estates and the silver birches and the uneven pavement. It did not surprise him that he now knew where he was. He walked slowly and breathed evenly. As he turned into his street someone brushed past him. The detective caught a confident smile on the face of the man who had jostled him. He was at his front gate when he realized that the smile belonged to the murder suspect. But when he turned to look the man was gone. There was an envelope pinned to his front door. Inside the envelope was a message composed of letters cut out of newspapers and magazines. The message read:

All alternative realities are true.

The detective let himself into his flat, shut the door behind him, and poured himself a glass of Argentinian Altamira. He sat down at a table near a window to contemplate the letter. After a while he brought out a worn book of Escher drawings. Leaving the doors in his mind open, he contemplated the drawings. But in the other rooms in his mind, he was thinking.

In his research he had discovered that the murder suspect had an unusual interest in a branch of speculative physics. In one room in his mind he realized that the solution to the crime was not to be found in the real world, but in an unreal space, a speculative realm. In another room, he pondered the message he had received. All alternative realities are true. He contemplated the ramifications of the message while leafing through the drawings. Calmly, he began charting out the clear lines of the case. Soon he came to a dead end. He paused, and put down the book.

He knew that all dead ends are an illusion designed to bring motion to a halt. To those who can see beyond the illusion, dead ends are portals into unknown possibilities. He paid more attention to dead ends than to open highways. He knew now that a leap of faith was required. Then he remembered the cat that was both seen and not seen. He realized he was going to have to work backward. He went to sleep that night with the feeling that he had at least stopped the multiplication of the problem.

3

The next morning, an envelope was posted through his letter box. Before he opened it he knew that he would find letters cut out of newspapers and magazines composing an elusive message.

The envelope contained a single sheet of white paper with the words:

The world is still here.

He had a shower, got dressed, and regarded his face in the mirror. The mirror had a slight warp that morning. He was not sure that the world was still there.

Outside, the weather had changed. The sun shone intermittently through dark masses of clouds. A cool wind, with a deceptively icy core, blew from the south. He went down side streets toward the café where the victim, Barrett, had been seen reading a cat.

The café was run by a long-haired Italian who combined obsequiousness with a mildly intrusive personal charm. Sitting in the same seat where the victim had been seen reading a cat, Detective Draper saw the canal beyond the balcony. There were boats moored on both sides. The detective drank his hot water slowly. He had given up drinking coffee years ago and had now settled for the digestive refinements of hot water. Outside, birds were wheeling over the canal.

While sipping, he had a singular thought. He knew that entertaining it would create realities that would only blur the case further, so he pushed the thought to a corner of his mind. He caught a taxi back to the office.

To test his theory he had his contact at the *Evening Standard* plant a report that the police were draining an obscure canal in Richmond in their search for the missing body. To lend this deception the veneer of plausibility, he had two amateur frogmen busily explore the canal. They were to pretend to pull something out of its shallow depths.

"What's the idea behind this flagrant waste of public funds on sham frogmen in a remote canal?" asked his superintendent who had summoned him to lunch. "You are aware that I have gone out on a limb for you too many times . . ."

"And I have never let you down, have I?" Detective Draper replied, calmly buttering his roll.

"No, you haven't, I grant you that, but there are many people after your job. They will use anything to get at you. God knows you have enough disadvantages as it is."

"Do I?" Detective Draper said, while the glimmer of a new thought flitted through a door in his mind.

"You know you do. You are not an Oxbridge man."

"Neither are you . . ."

"You are . . ."

"Black?"

"I wasn't going to say that."

"But you thought it."

"Look, we run the most . . ."

"Color-blind department in the country."

"You took the words right out of my mouth."

"But I am the only one that is . . . ?"

"We have to face the realities of the world."

Detective Draper suddenly stiffened. He held his head at an angle. A new thought had come through. "Do we?" he said absentmindedly.

"Yes, we do," replied the superintendent, puzzled by Draper's behavior.

"Have you had this conversation with me before?"

"That's what I was getting to."

"About an hour ago?"

"Yes. Why?"

"We don't have any time. We have to stop it now."

"Stop what?"

"There will be another murder unless we act fast."

"Murder? Of who?"

"The woman. She'll be murdered and there will be no evidence of it."

"Why not?"

"Because she would have been murdered yesterday." Detective Draper stood up.

"You're not making sense, man," the superintendent exploded. "Sit down, and explain yourself."

"I really must dash, sir. I'll have a full explanation for you tomorrow afternoon, if all goes well."

"But tomorrow is Saturday!" the superintendent said to the departing figure of the detective. "Yorkshire are playing Middlesex at the Oval."

"I know," Draper said, before he disappeared through the door, "and the score will be seventeen to one."

"What?" cried the superintendent.

Detective Draper was already out on the street.

4

From the Kensal Rise police station, Detective Draper requisitioned three frogmen. Early on Saturday morning he had them dive into the canal at Little Venice, right near the café. The area was cordoned off. The frogmen, in their dark wetsuits, began their mysterious exploration. There was a unit of police there, with an unmistakable police van. Detective Draper watched from a distance. If his intuition was correct, in the next hour a number of things would happen. Their precise order interested him. He knew he was in the realm of a speculative space now, where actually seeing what was sought made its existence real. The time, the opportunity, were limited. Things were in mutant formation. Events were hovering between two realms, between being and nonbeing. From here on the operation would be delicate.

The frogmen in the obscure canal at Richmond found nothing, as was the intention. But the story planted in the

Evening Standard had its desired effect, as far as the detective could tell. He kept looking at his watch. The frogmen here at the Little Venice canal took turns going in. One of them would stand on the edge of the canal and then flip over backward. He would root around below for a while and then emerge. For an hour now they had been exploring and had found nothing. The cricket game had begun at the Oval. The heat was beginning to rise. It was a bright day and people had begun to stop to watch the strange proceedings on the canal. This too had been factored into Detective Draper's complex calculation of events. Only by the frogmen diving, verifying, and bringing up, could there be anything to dive for, verify, and bring up. The detective knew this. Something will be found only because something is looked for. The looking creates the finding.

In just the same way, only the presence of onlookers created the event. The onlookers were essential. The detective had surmised that what was needed was a weighting of events toward a more dense reality, to counterbalance the ambiguous reality between worlds which had so far bedeviled the investigation. He intuited that all worlds had to come together here. That was why even before he had full permission, he'd arranged for the frogmen to make a public exhibition of excavating the muddy depths of the canal.

The ruse had worked. The item planted in the *Evening Standard* had caught the lively interest of Londoners and soon everyone was talking about it. The crowd around the canal observing the frogmen grew in number. The trap sprung had yielded multidimensional fruit. An off-duty policeman had spotted the suspected murderer near the Little Venice canal and had reported the matter to the local police station. The station chief had relayed the message to Detective Draper. With a nonchalant expression, he continued to observe the frogmen at work.

Twice the frogmen claimed to have found nothing. They had said it was just mud and rotting bicycles and broken paddles down there.

The detective, with his keen awareness of the power of numbers, said: "Twice does not make anything conclusive. The canal conceals secrets which must be exposed. My career depends on it. Maybe even my life."

He sent the frogmen down a third time. He suggested they look not so much in the deeper parts, but in the parts no one would think of looking.

"What part is that, sir?" one of the frogmen said.

"You will know when you find it."

Disgruntled, they returned to work. They flipped over backward, and disappeared beneath the muddied surface. Detective Draper, aware of the proximity of the murderer, knew that it was now a race against time. The frogmen had to find something before the murderer found him. He remained calm. He ordered a cup of hot water from the café. The café manager, the insouciant Italian, brought the water himself. His disheveled locks fell across his face. The

Italian handed the detective the cup of hot water and held onto the pot.

"So what is going on, sir?" the café manager asked.

Detective Draper turned to look at him. The Italian had the eyes of an insomniac. "It's best you don't know. We don't want you entangled in the multiple webs of the problem."

"I might be able to help."

"How?"

"I hear things. People tell me things."

"I'm sure that's true. I'll contact you if your help is required."

"Any time," said the Italian. "It would be an honor to be of service."

The café manager stood there watching the first frogman emerge from the murky canal. The detective turned to him with a furrowed brow and the Italian immediately understood that his presence had become redundant. He filled the detective's cup and retreated into his café.

Detective Draper felt the murderer moving closer, but he sipped his hot water with perfect calm. It is not the number of encounters in the numberless realms that count, it is the world in which the encounter is fixed, thought the detective grimly. A flurry among the frogmen told him that the nature of the game had shifted at last. He drank what was left of his hot water and went toward them.

One of the frogmen had pulled out from the depths of the canal a black plastic bag. Dripping with muck, it was placed on the ground. The frogmen hosed it down and then the detective had it brought to the back of the van. A casual glance at its form told him what he needed to know. There was no need to expose the contents. The first stage of the duel had been fought. It might have been difficult to fix the reality of this black dustbin bag, but now that it was fixed the rest were sure to be found. It was at that moment, perhaps delayed by the variable factors in the calculations of time, that a shadow moved into sight.

Jorg fired two shots. One shot pierced the metal of the white van, the other grazed Detective Draper's shoulder. Then Jorg was wrestled to the ground by the plainclothes policemen who had been drinking cups of innocuous tea in the café. Before the detective fell, he was heard to cry out: "On no account are the frogmen to cease their exploration!"

He passed out for only a few moments. An act of will wrenched him back into consciousness. Detective Draper allowed the paramedics to bandage his shoulder, while he surveyed the scene before him. The frogmen had persisted and eventually they had dredged up three black bin liners from diverse parts of the canal. They were hosed down and kept in the back of the van that the bullet had pierced. The detective had no need to inspect their contents. He knew what they were.

The afternoon sun played on the water of the canal, making its surface shine like gunmetal. The light came through the trees on both sides of the metal fences. Detective Draper could see the church through the leaves. He felt tired. He made a signal to one of the men. They bore him to a waiting car, but instead of being taken to the hospital for further treatment, he insisted on being taken home.

5

The next morning, with his arm in a sling, Detective Draper was at the police station. Out of respect for the part he had played in the investigation, he was allowed the first conference with the man who had shot him. They were in a soundproof room. The detective sat on a chair at the table and the murderer sat opposite.

"Something puzzles me," said Jorg. There was nothing repentant about his expression. He stared at the detective intensely.

"You want to know how I knew where to look?"

Jorg smiled. It was a thin smile, sustained by something resembling a twitch. Then he nodded faintly.

"My question to you is why?"

"Why what?"

They were still dueling. It was not over yet.

There was still the chance for further multiplications. He had to be careful.

"Why did you kill him?"

"Are you sure it is why and not when?"

"I know when."

"You do?"

"You are not going to trap me that easily again."

"I have no idea what you mean."

"Of course you do. All alternative realities are true."

"I see. You got the clue."

"It was designed to throw me off the scent."

"You went against your own psychology."

"Like you, I have many psychologies," the detective said, leaning back. "But why did you kill him?"

"He was after my woman."

"She was not your woman. She told the police that you were just her neighbor and that you had misunderstood her friendship."

"She was a whore and he deserved to die. He was not even one of us."

"You killed him out of jealousy."

"Not jealousy. Revenge."

The detective stood up. He felt weary. He was at the door when Jorg fired the last question at him.

"How did you know?"

The detective at that moment felt a throb of pain in his shoulder. "The world is still here," he replied, and went out.

6

Three hours later he was sitting with the superintendent in the Scotland Yard canteen. They had window seats looking out over the river.

"The facts don't make sense. Can you make sense of them for me, so I can explain it to the board?"

"I don't recommend an explanation."

"What then?"

"Leave them with the facts. Sometimes people need to be brought face-to-face with the incomprehensibility of the world."

The superintendent stared at him. "Now you know why you will never make department head."

"It never was my ambition."

"You have ambitions?"

"I have ambitions that perhaps you won't understand," said the detective, sipping his hot water. "Besides, there are things better than ambition."

"How can you stand to drink that tasteless stuff?"

"It's not tasteless at all. It restores me to the fundamental simplicity of the world."

"The world seems to be anything but simple. Take this case for example. What on earth was going on?"

"It wouldn't make sense if I explained it."

"Try me."

"It was a multiverse murder."

"What on earth is that? Speak plain English, man!"

"It was a murder that happened in many universes."

"You must be mad."

"In one universe the murder hadn't happened yet. In another, it had. Each time we apprehended him, we multiplied—"

"Okay, that's enough of that. If I hear any more I might start to have crackpot ideas myself. Just tell me this. Why the canal?"

"I realized it when I learned the victim was seen in the café reading a cat."

"Reading a cat?"

"The policeman who saw him was dyslexic. His condition was extreme. He saw visually what he read. About one percent of dyslexics have this syndrome."

"What was the cat he was reading?"

"It was a book. The book gave me the second clue. The rest unraveled itself."

"Out with it, man. You are tying me up in riddles. What was the book?"

"*Schrödinger's Cat.*"

"Schrödinger's what?"

"He had bought the book that morning and was seen reading it in the café after he had been murdered. Unless we were dealing with apparitions, there could only be one solution."

The superintendent looked red-faced and exasperated.

"I had to somehow get all the universes in which the murder was multiplying to converge. I had to create what physicists call an event convergence."

"What on earth is that?" bellowed the superintendent, by now a swollen image of himself.

"It is the one event, the one thing, that will fix time. In quantum mechanics, it is conjectured that the universe only comes into existence when we perceive it. I surmised that perhaps the body of the victim would only be found when we find it. The crime did not exist till the body was found."

"And the body was in the bin bags?"

"Exactly."

"How did you know?"

"One of the watchers outside the woman's house had seen the murder suspect cutting up a chicken."

"It was a chicken."

"It was a chicken because the watcher had seen a chicken."

"Do you mean to say—"

"Yes."

The superintendent paused for a long moment. "But why was he trying to kill you?"

"He wasn't really. We have to understand that this man was taking a cosmic gamble. He never really had any intention of killing anybody. He was overcome with rage, with jealousy, with a kind of love madness. In that state it occurred to him that maybe if he killed the man in one universe, the man would still be alive in another. Somewhere along the line he forgot what universe he was in. In short, he lost his reason."

"You mean he went mad?"

"Depends on what you think madness is."

"Continue."

"In one of those universes it occurred to him that if he

could stop me before I could find the body, then he would never be caught and the murder would to all accounts be forever speculative."

"Why wasn't I told all this at the time?"

"You were at your cricket match, sir."

"A terrible game. We were mauled."

"Sorry to hear that, sir."

"Still, you could have sent me a message."

"It was a delicate matter."

"What does that mean?"

"I had to arrive at the body before his bullet arrived in me."

There was a long pause.

"Detective Draper, you look terrible," the superintendent said. "When was the last time you had some sun?"

"Can't remember, sir."

"Get some sun. I want that shoulder working when you get back. Take a holiday, Detective Draper."

"Thank you, sir," the detective said, with a wry smile. "I think I might. While the world is still here."

The Story in the Next Room

We were in the big room. Next door, in the small room, was a young lady. She had been by herself for a long time.

"Why don't we ask her to tell us a story?" someone said.

"Why would she want to tell a story?" I said.

"Just ask her."

"Why should I ask her?"

"Go on."

I went next door and knocked. I thought I heard her say come in. I went in and saw her sitting on the bed. She was young and fair-skinned and had full fluffy hair. For a moment I found it hard to speak. She looked at me and said nothing. I said: "Would you come next door and tell us a story?"

"Why?"

"Why not?"

I knew why not. She was shy. She had the shyness of youth. It was a shyness that was also an affectation.

"Come on," I said. "What would it cost you?"

"I can't."

"Why not?"

"You know why not."

"Come on."

I saw it now as a challenge. I didn't need to. They had asked me to ask her, and now I wanted to see if I could get her to do it. I pleaded with her. She wouldn't budge.

I became aware that they were watching us through the little pane of glass. I could see their faces crowded into the square pane, watching to see if I would succeed.

She kept looking at me. I could see that her shyness wouldn't let her do it, but I kept asking her anyway. At last she said: "I won't come and tell a story, but I'll do this."

Then she took off her top. I tried not to look. They were fresh and small.

"Come next door and tell us a story. We'd like that. What would a story cost you anyway?"

"I just can't," she said.

She regarded me with gray-blue eyes. The faces were still pressed close to the semifrosted glass. I pleaded with her once more, but she was looking down at the black top in her lap.

"I wish I could, but I can't," she said, still looking down.

Maybe I shouldn't go on pleading with her, I thought. She doesn't want to tell a story. It's not easy telling a story. Most people would do anything rather than tell a story. Maybe I should leave her alone.

But now she was staring at me. It seemed like a challenge. I didn't move, but nor did she.

"Why don't you tell me a story," she said.

"Me?"

"Yes."

She gestured to the faces pressed to the glass, and they all came in. They sat on the bed.

"He's going to tell us a story," she said.

I hadn't noticed when she put her top back on. They were all looking at me. It was quite frightening. They looked as if they were going to devour me. I had to tell them a story. I took a deep breath.

"One day," I said, "I walked out my front door, and saw a tiger . . ."

The Overtaker

We were traveling through forests of iroko and baobab, over wooden bridges, on pitted tarmac roads. We had seen the wreckage of many accidents. Dad was driving.

We drove through the night, across the country. Owls swooped at us, illuminated by the headlights. Sinister goats watched us. A solitary woman, a bundle on her head, appeared in our headlights, and vanished into darkness.

Dad drove through the night and into the dawn. On the second day of our journey a Peugeot sped past us, blasting its horn.

"The race is not to the swift, nor the battle to the strong," Dad quoted.

Then we heard a thunderclap. Five minutes later we saw that the Peugeot was joined in a twisted embrace with a minibus. The Peugeot was mangled, its windscreen smashed and spiked with blood, its wheels still turning.

A woman wailed beneath the wreckage. A crowd had gathered, uttering low lamentations. Where had they emerged from? There was nothing but thick forest all around. Were they grief that had turned into human form?

Women struggled down from the back of the minibus, covered in blood and shards of broken glass.

Two men were on the ground, twitching. Their faces were damaged beyond recognition. Their arms and legs didn't look right. Two others were dead in the front seat of the Peugeot. It was impossible to extricate them from the wreckage.

Red dust hung like a cloud over the scene. The smell of blood mingling with the odor of gasoline was heavy in the torpid air.

The driver of the minibus was not one of the dead. The survivors of the accident kept asking for him, but he could not be found. His assistant, who was really a boy, threw himself on the ground, and wailed for his dead master.

"Where's the driver?" I heard people shout, but all the assistant did was wail.

It was a terrible crash and it made a great impression on me, like being struck by the lightning of life. I wandered among the dead bodies and stared with horror at the smashed vehicles.

The assistant began howling. A woman with blood dripping down her forehead kept walking around and around in a circle, muttering something to herself. The assistant kept saying it was impossible that his master was dead.

"What did he look like?" asked strangers who were trying to wrench open the driver's door.

No one could get any sense out of the assistant. At last he sat by the roadside, covered in dust. Someone poured a bottle of water on his head. With blank eyes he said we would recognize the driver by a scar running down his cheek, from his ear to his mouth.

"He was the greatest driver in Africa!" the assistant kept saying. "He was the fastest! He was the best!"

"But where is he?" the strangers asked. "There is no one in the driver's seat."

The assistant stared at them blankly.

"You think you will find him there? You think you will find him? He has strong juju. You won't find him!"

"But we must find him," the strangers said.

The assistant didn't seem to hear them. "We used to call him the overtaker! He could overtake anything! Now my master, my great master, is dead!"

There was much wailing. Wounded mothers with their wounded children were prostrate in the dust.

There was the stench of blood evaporating on hot crumpled metal. Seeking relief from the wailing, I wandered away from the smash.

The air was hot, the dust red, and the aroma of the forest was sticky. The road glimmered with heat. I listened to long drawn-out birdcalls.

I got to a makeshift wooden bridge. A man was sitting on its edge, his leg swinging in the air, nearly touching the metal-gray water.

The bridge had been worn down by heavy-haulage lorries and no repairs. Its railing had long been damaged by cars and lorries that had plunged over in thoughtless haste. There were rotting vehicles and jutting boulders in the river. The boulders were like the backs of prehistoric animals asleep in the sun.

The man sitting on the edge was looking at the corpses of cars and at the clear swiftly flowing water. He was smoking a pipe. It did not smell like tobacco. It smelled like burning flesh. There was something serene about the man which disturbed me. I was beginning to turn back when he said: "Boy, come here."

I did not move.

"I said come here!"

Still I did not move.

"What are you doing here?" he said with a smile.

Something was not right about his smile.

"I don't know," I said, with a dry throat. "There was an accident."

"So you walked away from an accident?"

"No."

"What did you do then?"

"I don't know."

"Do you know anything?"

I didn't know what to say. He drew on his pipe, but blew out no smoke. The sun was harsh, but he did not sweat. The heat did not touch him. The wind that came from the forest brought no coolness. I began to leave, when he said: "It's good to look at the water."

His words made me look. The river rushed over rocks and wrecked cars.

"It's good to sit on a bridge and smoke a pipe."

His voice made me want to sit on the edge and be closer to the water.

"It's good to take things easy and go gently."

I was bewitched by the simplicity of his words. I was mesmerized by the silence. Then he turned his face to me. There was something not quite right about his face.

"Who is your father?"

"He's a lawyer."

"Where is he going?"

"He's driving us home?"

"What home?"

"Our home in the city."

"Is there a home in the city?"

I didn't understand what he was getting at. I stayed silent. After a while he smiled again. The smile did not brighten his face.

"Come here," he said.

I went closer.

"Give your father this message," he said, almost in a

whisper. "Tell him to go slowly. To take things easy. These roads are lonely and want blood."

He paused.

"Home is wherever you are happy."

He looked at me with strange eyes.

"Tell your father what I just told you."

I didn't move. Something about his face held me.

"Go away now!" he shouted suddenly. "Go back to your father!"

I was rooted.

"Leave this bridge now! Don't stare into the water!"

I was unable to move.

"Leave now before I change my mind," he said, smiling again.

His smile frightened me and I turned and stumbled and nearly fell through the wide gap in the railings. I stopped myself and ran and fell and got up again, my head spinning.

I ran all the way back into the arms of my father, jabbering about a message I was supposed to give him. The women gave me water to drink.

We stayed there till the wounded were borne off to the nearest hospital. About the dead not much could be done.

As we pulled away I gave Dad the message. We passed the bridge but there was no one there.

The boulders in the river were smooth in the sun.

Raft

It was crowded on the raft. It was a small raft but the man had said it would carry us to Greece. Halfway across, it began listing.

There were too many of us on the raft. Many of us sat on the edge. Many families were hunched in the middle where it sagged. The water was rough and many of us threw up.

There were women with babies, men with wives, families with bundles. The sea was rough. Sometimes the wave lifted us high and dashed us back down and a cry would rise from the men and women. Sometimes the raft would spin and there was nothing we could do but pray, or howl.

There were two life jackets. When the raft got too full and the sea got too rough we would see that someone had fallen off. We would try to get ahold of them and give them a life jacket.

We were halfway across the diamond-blue sea when someone cried: "The water is above our ankles!"

Then we saw that the raft was leaking. We didn't have anything to bail the water out. Someone was using a small Evian bottle to bail out the water. The water kept rising.

Babies were crying. Women were wailing. The men were shouting. Overhead white birds were keening.

The waves were rough. We were crowded in the raft and the raft was leaking. Soon the water was at our knees and we were sliding into the sea.

We sat on the edge leaning back. Many of us were sick because we could not swim. The land was still far away. There was no horizon and no land to be seen. A yacht sailed by on the edge of the blue sea.

The raft was sinking. The women were wailing. We were crowded in water rising up to our waists. There were men in the water clinging to the raft and wearing life jackets. There was no space on the raft. The women and children were in the sea, and the sea was in the raft.

We had run out of prayers. Our feet were no longer in the raft but in the sea.

Then there was a whirling sucking sound.

The Secret History of a Door

When Newgate Prison was torn down its brick and metal were scattered all over London. The scaffold on which people were hanged was burned. It was said that the cries of innocent victims could be heard in the crackling smoke from that blood-soaked wood.

Nobody knew what to do with one of the strangest things in that infamous prison. No one knew what to do with the door. It was an imposing door of solid metal. It had rectangular holes, like little windows. It bristled with metal studs, and had a huge bolt.

It was said that when criminals were led into the prison they maintained their bravado till they beheld this door. It has been claimed that the door was cursed with the power to freeze the hearts of evil men.

In front of the door the innocent experience a sense of lightness, and after it has been bolted behind them the sound of the clanging metal brings them a welcome, if brief, benediction.

But to murderers, child molesters, and corrupt politicians the door represents hell itself. When the bolts are shot behind them darkness falls over their lives.

For over a hundred years the door has looked upon all manner of men and women. It has absorbed all the permutations of evil that can sprout and fester in the cancerous hearts of man. The door has grown solid with evil, muted with grief, heavy with sin.

Theosophists believe that objects absorb the emotions of lives in close proximity to them. This door, which could not be burned and could not be broken apart, became the most terrifying testimony of the depths to which the human heart can sink. When Newgate Prison was destroyed no one knew what to do with this great metal door which was its heart.

2

The door was forgotten in a heap somewhere in the city. Where it lay strange things blossomed. It became the gateway through which the spirits of executed criminals could, for a time, return to the world that had left them behind. They roamed the city, brooding on vengeance.

Historians maintain that in ancient Egyptian tombs there are false doors through which the ka of the dead can return to the world and eat the offering left for them by the living. This discarded door of Newgate Prison was the door of the criminal dead.

At night the spirits of infamous highway robbers, cutthroats, rapists, and arsonists found their way through this neglected door, and spread waves of criminal thoughts throughout the unsuspecting city. The police were mystified at the sudden rise of old-fashioned crimes. It was as though criminal gangs had an unprecedented wave of inspiration from long-forgotten generations of their fraternity. It seemed to the police that old gangs, lurking in the underworld, had now resurfaced.

There were murders and shadow murders all across the city. Reports of the number of ghost sightings of highwaymen rose dramatically. A boy's testimony was luridly illustrated in all the papers. He claimed to have seen a dead man with a noose around his neck emerging from an abandoned door. Psychics, spiritualists, and exorcists converged on the door and it didn't take them long to unanimously pronounce it monstrous.

"This is the most evil door in the land," a priest said.

"This is the most pain-soaked door in the land," a famous medium declared.

Those who lived near the door claimed that at night they could hear cries coming from it, the cries of those who seemed shut up in hell. The clanging and bolting shut of metal haunted the dark hours. The broken howl of decapitation pierced the East End nights.

3

Artists were drawn to the door. Its solid abstract shape, the pattern of its grille, its nocturnal green, and its pullulating metal studs inspired canvases with unexpected images. Artists composed some of their most infernal paintings under the aegis of its power. They claimed that something seemed to take over their hands while working. One or two artists who painted the door never painted again.

Poets found in the door a romantic image of the criminal spirit. They wrote long Byronic poems about the grimness of the fetter and the unbounded dream of freedom and about unknown doors to the underworld. One or two poets who wrote poems about the door succumbed to fatal addictions and disappeared from their respectable lives in society. One of them took to the highway and was shot dead at night by an exasperated police force. Another poet, whose case was much celebrated in the press, worked on an epic poem about the door for over seventy-two hours without a break and was found dead in his bathrobe with a bottle of absinthe at the foot of his table. The poem was destroyed by his widow. Some of the poets who wrote about the door never wrote poems again, but worked diligently in the advertising industry.

All those who came into contact with the door acknowledged there to be something weird about it. In its vicinity all things were touched by a dark enchanted power.

Innocent objects within its radius took on sinister aspects. Around it crawled a torrid spectral life.

4

Then one day something happened which changed the fate of the door.

Children were playing nearby. They were playing games of war, games of fugitive and policemen, of hide-and-seek. One of the boys hid beneath the door and was never found again. He was a particularly bright boy. He was good at mathematics and had a gift for healing wounded animals. After his disappearance the hauntings by criminals ceased and the tide of old-fashioned crimes waned and fell away altogether.

The Offering

*For a long time I wanted to see them. I had heard about them
in my childhood in the tales my father told in the evenings
with his face turned toward the mountains. My mother had
told me stories about them too with woodsmoke in the air.
Often when I fell asleep I thought I saw them. But I didn't
see them. For many years I heard no more tales about them.
My mother took her tales with her to the grave and I went
away to school where they told no tales about such things.*

*The years were long. I traveled far and went to other
lands that were colder than this. Their tales were frozen tales
about girls in ice palaces. All through my travels I longed for
woodsmoke tales.*

*I had long finished my studies. I worked now as an an-
thropologist. But I cared for none of this. I was still that girl
who longed to see them.*

This summer I decided to take a journey up into the

mountains. *Maybe something was calling me. I went to that region where they say you can see them. It is an enchanted region high up in the Andes. The people there are poor and their lives are simple. As I ascended the ranges into their villages I knew I had entered a different kind of space.*

There were many legends here about them. They said you could see them by the lakes or under the waterfalls. I went walking by the lakes barefoot. All along the shores I saw guitars. They were laid out with a bunch of red or yellow flowers beside them. There were places where I saw guitars on a stone, in the sun, by the river. They seemed like offerings.

Sometimes I heard a ghostly strumming across the lakes and I longed to cross over to see what it was that produced such unearthly music. The villagers told me it was wise not to make such a crossing, that those who crossed over never came back.

They spoke of musicians who came to the lakes hoping to see them. They came with their musical instruments and made offerings and tuned their guitars under the waterfall hoping for the gift of that otherworldly inspiration. Many musicians had died here seeking the gifts of the elusive ones.

I did not eat much in the time I was there. Something about the mood of the place made eating unnecessary. I was not a musician but I wanted the elusive ones to tune my instrument, whatever that might be. I woke early and walked barefoot and carried a yellow flower in my hand in case I saw one of them.

Before dawn, the music from across the lakes was almost too sweet to bear. I alone heard it. The sun then was like a smear of butter on the horizon. Soon the hills would quiver and melt with that celestial furnace. Only the lakes would be cool.

Like a deserted habitation of musicians, the guitars left on the shores and on the rocks glistened with dew. I made no footprints on the virgin shores. The lake at that hour seemed especially enchanted. It was a mountain lake and the first time you rose from the climb and saw it you felt as if you were beholding a miracle. A cry escaped from my lips that made something near me that I couldn't see flutter and leap back into the water. I saw nothing but the closing of the water's face. There was something unnerving about the way the water closed its face.

From that moment on my nerves were on edge. It felt like a slow madness was creeping into me. I had the sense of a giant cockatoo just beyond the edge of my vision. I had the sense of someone walking beside me, listening to my thoughts.

It was good to suddenly hear music when I felt like that. It was as if someone had diverted a thread of the waterfalls through my being. I felt on the edge of seeing things not of this world. I was on the edge a long time, for days and weeks, and never quite going over.

Maybe it was my training that held me back. I wanted to lose all I had learned on those shores. The morning was fresh with the fragrance of legends. The blue mountain lakes were like mint to the eyes. There was so much beauty to see that I could not see. There were drugs I would happily have taken to release me from my bondage.

After the third week, I began to wonder what I was doing there. I was beginning to think of going back down when an old man told me the legend of a secret lake higher up in the mountains.

"I know what you seek," he said. "Many have sought it too and have left with nothing. Only those musicians devoted beyond death itself, willing to lose their minds to the harsh goddess of this place, ever find the new sound that their souls crave. Mostly they leave with a new subject or at best some inflection of a mountain riff. I am a musician myself. I am one of those who came to offer my guitar to those who cannot be seen to tune my instrument to a new inspiration that through me may be renewed the soul and temper of the Americas. Some days I thought I had found it, and a strange sound floated across the waters when I played. But after many years I realized that it was merely the altitude, and that I was hearing my old familiar self in these rarefied airs. Then one day I saw what I sought. She touched my guitar and it went mute forever. I could not return to the world with a mute song. So I stayed here and slowly I am becoming part of the stone and part of the shore. Look at my arms, plants are growing on me. This is what it means to seek unknown revelations. Do you still want to know of this secret lake?"

"Yes," I said, taken aback by the waterfall of his speech.

"Not many people in these regions know of it. To see it alone is a sign of some sort of spiritual favor. But you won't know the source of this favor till maybe it is too late. There you will find what you seek."

"How do you know what I seek?"

"I know the hunger and the derangement in those eyes. Mine were like yours once."

It gave me a shiver to hear him say that.

"Not many women seek what you seek."

"Really?"

"The ones that do have run away from the furnace of the world."

"Do they find what they seek?"

"Not one that I have heard of."

"Has anyone?"

"No."

"What happens to them?"

"They become part of the legends."

I had no more questions and stood silently staring into the sky. It was then that he described the special path I must take, and the special rituals I must make, to find the secret lake.

The next morning early, I set off. White birds with yellow beaks were on the wind. Wisps of an anguished guitar melody sounded from a half-open door. My footsteps echoed on the face of the lake. I walked for a long time toward the rising heat. There were moments when my head swayed and I felt as if I had drunk a barrel of raw beer. Sometimes I forgot myself and it was as if the road were walking me. By the early afternoon I arrived and my feet were blistered and the altitude made my nerves jumpy. I had arrived but I still could not see this secret lake that the old man had spoken about.

I went on walking till I saw a boy playing by the path. I asked him about the secret lake and he smiled as if he were expecting me. Before I had finished he jumped up on his feet and with an excited half walk, half run led me around many turns, through narrow spaces in the mountains where the rocks grazed my face, through a field of sorrel. I saw flowers I have never seen before.

"Can you not see it?" I suddenly heard the boy say.

I looked up but saw nothing. The boy was ahead of me. I followed him at a run.

I certainly did not want to lose him now, after all the heat blisters on my face. I saw him turn the corner of a misshapen rock. When I went around the rock I could have fallen into it.

There it was, in the palm of the mountains, a pristine silvery-blue lake that only time had breathed on. Slowly, across its face, birds inscribed their arcane alphabets. Here was not the legend, but the source of legends itself.

The boy was not looking at the lake, nor at me. It was a moment before I realized he was looking beyond me. I turned and saw nothing. Then I heard a delayed splash in the lake right near where I was standing.

"Did you see her?"

"Who?"

"Her."

"Who?"

"The woman of the water. Didn't you see her?"

"No."

"You were looking at her."

"Was I?"

"And she was looking at you."

"I didn't see her."

"I thought you knew her."

"Why do you say that?"

"The way you were looking at her. She knew you."

"How do you know?"

"The way she was smiling at you."

"She was smiling at me?"

"Yes. I think she likes you."

"Now you are talking nonsense."

"Didn't you see the sign she made you?"

"What sign?"

He made the sign. It was an invitation, a call, a summons.

"Was that the sign?"

"Yes. She made it once."

"Once."

"Yes. I have never heard of her doing that before."

"Really?"

"Yes. I think she likes you."

"Thank you."

"It's nothing."

He stayed a moment. I gave him a coin. He took it and ran off back to the village. I sat by the shore, at the exact spot where the boy had seen her. I stared a long time at the lake. Then I took my clothes off and dived into the blue waters.

But when I dived in the water was gone. A woman stood there in the empty space where the lake had been and said: "I hear that you came here seeking something. What did you seek?"

"I wanted to see them."

"Who are them?"

"The elusive ones of the lake."

"What do you want from them?"

"I too want to tune my instrument to a new inspiration."

"Where is your instrument? The others leave their guitars on the shore or under the waterfall. Where is yours?"

"I am my instrum . . ."

When I show people pictures of the lake all they see are its pale blue and muted silver and the low ring of mountains.

They never see what I saw afterward.

Don Ki-Otah* and the Ambiguity of Reading

When he came into the printer's shop, we thought he was drunk. He had come to see for himself the machine that multiplies realities. He came in with his machete drawn. He had been passing by on one of his adventures to the North. He had heard that there was a war going on between giants and men. He wanted to fight against the giants. He claimed to have fought them before.

When he came into the shop he had the idea that the printing machine was in some way antagonistic to him. We had been working the shafts and the steel plates, applying oils and clearing the machine of impediments. He approached the machine as though it were a dangerous foe.

It took awhile to realize he wasn't drunk at all. He was

---

*He was known originally as Don Quixote, but under the imaginative force of African nicknaming he became Don Ki-Otah.

just rough in speech. He had a restless spirit and a bound-less imagination.

Conversation with him was difficult. He was liable to misunderstand the simplest thing you said. His companion, Sancho, seemed the only person who could calm him down. We asked Sancho to get him to drop his machete. But Sancho too had diabolical notions about the printing machine. We had two mad people in that tight space.

There have been many accounts of what happened when Don Ki-Otah stumbled into the first printer's shop he had ever encountered. Most of the accounts are lies. When an event passes into legend, people always claim they were there at the time. I was there when it happened. I was there.

"Let me see how it works!" Don Ki-Otah commanded, waving the machete close to my chin.

He stood over the machine, his eyes flashing. I noticed his beard for the first time. It was long and white and pointed. His eyes had great vigor. His proximity made the space around him charged. What it was charged with I cannot say.

"What would you like to see?" I asked.

"Print something."

"Anything?"

He gave me a sharp look.

"Yes."

I continued printing what was on the blocks. I worked

laboriously, sweating under the ferocity of his gaze. It was hard to work while he breathed down my neck. Eventually I pulled out some freshly printed pages.

"You have to wait for them to dry," I said.

"I will wait."

He still had the machete. His eyes made you think he was mad.

For him, waiting involved a special passion. I had never seen anyone wait with such intensity. It was as if by the force of his spirit he was regulating the motions of the moon or the subtle energies that flow through all things.

When a person is touched by greatness might it not be because they are resonating with this subtle energy that runs through spiders' webs and the intricate motion of the stars?

While he was waiting I noticed that he was concentrating on a crest of cobwebs in a high corner of the workshop. I was ashamed of the state of the place and became defensive.

"We clean the place once every we—"

He cut through my explanation with the sword of his wit. "If only," he said, with a glint in his eyes, "if only we knew the webs that connect us, it would be easier to send a message to the highest authorities with a tug of thought than by protesting at their gates."

He must have noticed the blankness of my look.

"I believe that the true warrior acts on the secret foundations of things, don't you?"

I gave him a look of incomprehension. The level at which he spoke was too elevated for me. Then I noticed something else about Don Ki-Otah. He was a walking encyclopedia of nonsense and wonders. While waiting he began a dissertation on the analogies between the spider's web and people's inability to alter the world. He philosophized while we waited. I couldn't make out much of what he said. I heard fall from his lips words like Amadís of Gaul, Plato, the Knights of the Arduous Road. He mentioned the tragedies of Sophocles, the last ironic paragraph of *Things Fall Apart*, and a fragment of Okigbo which he quoted again and again. Then he let fall a string of Luo proverbs, incanted a Swahili song, and strung out an Urhobo fable from which he drew threads of a luminous wisdom that held us spellbound.

When something extraordinary is happening in your life, time has a way of becoming an underwater phenomenon. It may be the distance of forty years, but there was a curious charm about those hours. It was a charm tinged with the old African magic one rarely encounters anymore. Sometimes one comes upon a seer emerging briefly from a long solitude in the forest. Don Ki-Otah was like one of those seers. Like a story made real for a moment, he came into our lives, and then he was gone.

Afterward all one heard of him were legends. He had waged battles with corrupt government officials, and embarked on campaigns in the forests of the North where

Boko Haram terrorized the nation. It was even rumored that he had been selected to join a resettlement program on Mars. These are stories his madness generated. It is hard to say whether his deeds exceeded our imagination, or whether we are poor reporters of the marvelous.

Let it be said, while I have breath, that he made us more imaginative, just by being himself. I had never felt myself more locked in the little box of my possibilities than in the presence of that man. He was a call to greatness. We failed to take up that challenge, cowards that most of us are. That failure is the lingering regret of my life. For a life passes, a life is lived. It is lived under fear and caution. One thinks of one's family. One thinks of one's self. But the life passes. And it is only the fires that your life lights in other people's souls that count. This I know now in the long uneventful autumn of my life. There are some people one should never have met, because they introduce into your heart an eternal regret for the greater life you did not live.

The paper dried, and when I was sure Don Ki-Otah would not have ink smudged on his face, I let him have what we had been printing. I did not know it would have the strange effect that it did.

He read the text very slowly. In all my life I have not met anyone who read more slowly. This puzzled me. It was because of reading too many books that he lost his mind. He couldn't have read so many books if he read so slowly.

"You are taking too much time with the reading," I said to him.

The tension in the room changed. Sancho, leaning his fat frame against the door, gasped. I did not understand the gasp and turned toward him. Then I felt the machete whizzing past my face, a cool breeze at the end of my nose. How calmly we regard extreme things after they have happened. I turned to Don Ki-Otah.

"Do you think," he said, manipulating his face into a most peculiar shape, "that I read 67,322 books by taking instructions from you—in how to read?"

The manner in which he spoke confused me. He made words sound more than they are. Other people say words and they mean less. He made words feel like more. He made your hairs stand on end when he spoke. I felt a furry growth at the side of my face when he addressed me. I stared at him, mesmerized.

"So you presume to tell Don Ki-Otah how to read?"

My mouth was dry.

"Pull up your ears! Clear them of wax! Get rid of that dim expression on your face! Stand up straight, young man, and listen!"

I drew breath. I felt faint. With a few syllables he could induce madness. His speech rocked the back of my skull. I don't know what came over me. One after the other, I pulled my ears. I tweaked them up straight like a rabbit's. All the while he stared at me with terrifying concentration. If he had carried on staring at me much longer I might have gone up in flames. I made an effort to stand up straight, till my head grazed the ceiling of his contempt.

"What did I say?" he bellowed. "Listen!"

I swallowed. It was a bruising adventure to be in his presence.

"In the course of a fifty-year reading career," he said, directing at me an unblinking focus, "I have experimented with 322 modes of reading. I have read speedily like a bright young fool, crabbily like a teacher, querulously like a scholar, wistfully like a traveler, and punctiliously like a lawyer. I have read selectively like a politician, comparatively like a critic, contemptuously like a tyrant, glancingly like a journalist, competitively like an author, laboriously like an aristocrat. I have read critically like an archaeologist, microscopically like a scientist, reverentially like the blind, indirectly like a poet. Like a peasant I have read carefully, like a composer attentively, like a schoolboy hurriedly, like a shaman magically. I have read in every single possible way there is of reading. You can't read the number and variety of books I have read without a compendium of ways of reading."

He stared at me. I felt he could see the inside of my head.

"I have read books backward and inside out. I began reading Ovid in the middle and then to the end and then from the beginning. I once read every other sentence of a book I knew well and then went back and read the sentences I missed out. We are all children in the art of reading. We assume there is only one way to read a book. But a book read in a new way becomes a new book."

I felt he was reading me as he spoke.

"And you have the nerve to tell me I am reading too slowly. Part of the trouble with our world, my snooty young friend, is that the art of reading is almost dead. Reading is the secret of life. We read the world poorly, because we read poorly. Everything is reading. The world is the way you read it. As we read, so we are. You are trying to read me now."

His focus on me made me nearly jump out of my skin. I could not read him. I would not even dare to begin. He was like a Chinese pictograph or a hieroglyph.

"Don't deny it. I can see your eyes wandering about my face as if it were an incomprehensible text."

He paused.

"You are even trying to read this moment in time. But you read it dimly. The words are not clear on the pages of your life. Youth clouds your seeing. Emotions pass in front of the text before you have grasped it. Can you read yourself in the chapter of time?"

He was staring at me again and all I had was muteness.

"You are a living paragraph of history. Around you are all the horrors of time and all the wonders of life, but all you see is an old man reading with all his soul. Do you know what I am reading?"

I shook my head, as if in a trance.

"I am reading a text by a Spaniard about my adventures in La Mancha."

He guessed at the vacuity of my grasp.

"You have no idea what I am talking about, and you dare to criticize how I read?"

Another short laugh burst out of him.

"I don't read slowly. And I have long ago left reading fast to those who will continuously misunderstand everything around them. I read now the way the dead read. I read with the soles of my feet. I read with my beard. I read with the secret ventricles of my heart. I read with all my sufferings, joys, intuitions, all my love, all the beatings I have received, all the injustices I have endured. I read with all the magic that seeps through the cracks in the air. Do you, therefore, dare to judge the way I read?"

"I'm sorry, sa," I murmured. "I did not mean anything..."

"You would prefer me to gulp words down like a drunk guzzling palm wine in a bukka?"

"No, sa."

"I suppose you think the faster you read, the more intelligent you are?"

"Not at all, sa."

In truth, though, this is what I believed.

"I suppose for you living fast is genius. I bet you fuck fast too. Fuck so fast that the poor woman has hardly had time to notice that you were in her."

"Not at all, sa!"

"Not at all, what?"

"I don't know, sa. I am confused, sa."

He inflicted on me another long stare. I felt myself shrink to a tiny form, one inch from the floor. At the same time I felt magnified beyond the sky. He had that paradoxical effect.

As he stared at me it seemed my life rushed before my eyes. I felt myself hurtling through time. I grew older, more arrogant, more successful. A chance event brought me down. Then years of doubt followed. My waistline thickened. I found a wife, became a father, and lost all my dreams. I worked hard in the name of raising a family. And then I was an old man on a porch, wondering where all the magic and promise of life had gone, when only yesterday I was a young apprentice with all the world before me. Then Don Ki-Otah comes into the printer's shop, and shakes my life with his mad Urhobo gaze.

"What you don't understand," he said, relentlessly, "is that nothing is done faster than when it is done well."

For the first time, I noticed the unnatural silence in the workshop.

"You read for information, I read to extract the soul of the conception. Reading is like entering the mind of the gods, seeing beyond the page. Can you read an entire history from a single glance? Can you deduce a poet's health or the station of their time here on earth from a single line of their poetry? You think reading is about reading fast. But reading is about understanding that which cannot be understood, which the words merely hint at."

He would have gone on in this fashion had Sancho not sneaked a look at the text that Don Ki-Otah had in his hands.

"My dear Don," said Sancho, "but I see your name on the pages you are reading. How did that come to be?"

Don Ki-Otah paused in a particularly brilliant crescendo of thought. Then he lashed Sancho with one of those gazes perfected in the creeks of Urhoboland.

"Did you not hear one word I've been saying to our young friend here about reading?"

"Don, the things you say are too intelligent for me. They go clean over my head. I watch them sailing past. I don't find it helpful to pay attention to what you say. But your name on these pages, what is it doing there?"

Don Ki-Otah brought the machete, flat surface down, hard on the edge of the printing machine. Sparks shot out into our faces. Don Ki-Otah was himself taken aback by the sparks. His eyes protruded.

I sensed another long speech coming on. To distract him, I said: "Aren't you going to continue with your reading?"

For a moment he was torn between a scientific and a literary choice. With a sigh, pulling at his beard as if it helped him concentrate, he returned to the text. He read in silence like a man drowning. A wall gecko ran halfway up the wall. The wall gecko saw Don Ki-Otah reading and was transfixed by the vision. I watched the wall gecko watching Don Ki-Otah. It must have been a historic sight.

Now, many years later, I see how much of a historic moment it was. It was a moment in which a golden line between the old and new time was crossed.

Can someone reading constitute a significant moment in the cultural life of a whole people? Can something so intimate have historical repercussions? I do not want to make extravagant claims for such a subjective activity. But what if the understanding of one mind precipitates the understanding of the many? There is a moment in the life of a people when things are suddenly seen for what they are. It may be injustice, or it may be a great social evil. But what if such a seeing was achieved first by one and then by the rest of us? Maybe the great historical moments, the storming of the barricades, the laws eradicating poverty, the liberation of women from servitude, the proclamation of racial equality, the protection of the earth's environment, are the outer forms of an inner activity. Maybe a people see first and then the realm of deeds comes after.

But as Don Ki-Otah read that text we could feel the air in the room change. His way of reading was like a prosecution of all our assumptions. It was like a thousand question marks scattered across our corruption-infested landscape. Even his face kept altering as he read. His beard was twisted into the enigmatic shapes of ancestral sculptures.

In the silence a thousand questions began to swim up to me. Maybe it was that long in-between time usually given up to chatter. Maybe it was the time used in covering up that which we do not want to see, but which stares at us like a corpse at the side of the street. Maybe it was that silence, so rare in our times, allowed the questions to rise up to the holes in the roof, through which they escaped out into the nation.

Being an eminently practical man, according to his own curious logic, Don Ki-Otah would disapprove of such fanciful notions. But something happened in that space, in that silence, as he sucked in the air with the concentration of his reading. It may have been the beginning of reading the world, reading the world in which we suffered every day. It was that more than anything.

He infected us with a new way of reading. We began to read the cockroaches. We read the spiders' webs. We read the raw roads and the corpses under the bushes. We read the cracks in our faces, through which despair seeped out. We read our extraordinary talent for evasion. We read our breathing and noticed what a pungent text the air made. When we began to read the shacks, the slums, and the palatial houses with armed guards and high electric fences, when we began to read those who grew fatter as we grew thinner, when we began to read the ambiguous text of our recent history, we saw that the world was not what we thought it was.

Before, we had seen the world as somehow inevitable. We had seen that it was the only way it could be. Now, with the new reading, we saw that the world was only one of a thousand ways it could be. But we had chosen this one, with its bad smells, its injustice.

All this happened in the space of a printed page. Don Ki-Otah read the page. Then he took up another printed page. He read that. Then he looked up. His head aslant, he regarded us with puzzlement.

"What is it?" Sancho said, rushing forward. He sensed distress in the eyes of his beloved master and friend.

"What is it? What is it? Have you seen what I am reading?"

"No. What is it?"

I don't know how, but he had ink on his face. He looked both comical and ghoulish. He misunderstood our collective stares. He seemed to think that we knew what he had been reading, and that we had somehow colluded in it. His machete rose above his head, and we backed off into the shadows, and pressed ourselves into the walls. The curve of our backs ought to have dented the bricks.

"These are pages about our adventures," he cried.

"What adventures?"

"All our adventures."

"All?"

"All since we left Ughelli and roamed the world as far as La Mancha, fighting demons, defeating giants, rescuing women from abduction, tilting at oil rigs, battling corruption. It's all here!"

"But how can that be? No one else knows of those adventures except us. I haven't told anybody. Have you?"

"Don't be silly, Sancho."

"But who is writing down those adventures? Is it someone we know?"

"Someone called Ben Okri. He claims to be writing the adventures from oral history."

"Oral history?"

"Yes, oral history. Don't look so stupid, Sancho. It is word-of-mouth history."

"You mean gossip?"

"Not just gossip."

"You mean rumor?"

"No. Stories told by people."

"Can you trust it?"

"Oral history can be more reliable than written history."

"You don't really believe that, do you?"

"Why not?"

"People exaggerate. They tell tall tales. Sometimes they engage in propaganda."

"I know. Oral history gives us the spirit, but written history gives us only the facts. The facts, by themselves, tell us very little."

"So are we to believe this Ben Okri?"

"He also claims to be writing the adventures from

manuscripts originally written by Cervantes, who wrote his from papers he discovered by Cide Hamete Benengeli, who got it from an Arabian manuscript."

"It sounds very complicated."

"It is not complicated at all. It is like biblical genealogy."

"What is genealolology? You are always using words bigger than me and I am a big man. Can you not find a simpler word for a plain man like me?"

"And that is not all," roared Don Ki-Otah, ignoring Sancho's request.

"There's more?"

"Of course there is more. Why else would I be so upset?"

"You are always upset about something. Or you are always upsetting something."

"Shut up, Sancho."

Sancho offered the Don a glum look.

"This fellow has written adventures I haven't had yet."

"You mean he has written your future?"

Don Ki-Otah considered this. His face was almost meditative. "He has written one future."

"How many futures are there?"

"We have a wise saying in our village. A man's future changes when he changes how he lives."

"Forgive me for being stupid, but is that not one of the futures too?"

"No!" bellowed Don Ki-Otah. "We believe that a person can confound their future. It was prophesied for me that I would die in my bed, and that I would renounce the life I have lived. But I will do no such thing."

"How do you know?"

"They can write my future. But I am the only one who can write my present."

"So you are going to become a writer now?"

"Of course not, Sancho. I have chosen to live. I have chosen the noble path of adventure, not the sedentary art of writing."

"You had me worried for a minute."

"When I say I will write my present I only mean that I will write it in how I live it. For many people, writing is what they do on a page. For a rare few, writing is what they do with life. Some write their texts on paper. I write my text on the living tissue of time. I write my legends on the living flesh of the present moment."

"I prefer pounded yam and egusi soup, with goat meat."

"Of course you do, Sancho."

"Each to his own."

"For me, however, all destiny is here. In this moment. This present moment is one the gods have no control over."

"Why not?"

"Because they have yielded to us the marvels of consciousness."

"I had never thought of that before."

"Of course you hadn't, Sancho. Most people read books; I read life. Some people write stories; I live them."

He looked around the workshop.

"Let's go," he said abruptly. "We have spent enough time in this house of embalmment." He slid the machete into a rough sheath that he wore at his side.

Moved to a defense of my apprenticeship as a printer's assistant, I cried: "Embalmment?" I did not even know what the word meant.

"Yes, embalmment," replied Don Ki-Otah, calmly. "What else are you doing here but burying living time in the tomb of print? What are you doing but fixing in the amber of print that which was fluid and multidimensional?"

Again I stared at him stupefied. My mind had a hundred objections, but my mouth was stuck.

He continued evenly: "This workshop is a graveyard of life. Life has a thousand colors, meanings, layers, aspects known and unknown. Print has only one face. That face, in a thousand years, is taken to be the only truth. This is a house of the falsifications of time. I will have nothing more to do with it."

"But we leave a record," I cried. "This is history!"

"The father of lies!" returned Don Ki-Otah, with unnatural tranquility.

The years pass and a great ambiguity falls over those words. The years pass and I become aware that we never really see what is there before us. It is as if the event veils its own truth.

It seems he could indeed read the future in a grain

of text. The truth is that after he left that day we scoured all the printed matter we had in the shop. We found that nothing we had printed that day or any other day bore any resemblance to that which he claimed he had read.

It began to dimly occur to us that maybe we did not know how to read the secret scripts of life concealed in the ordinary stuff we printed every day. It occurred to us that we did not know how to read at all. This was perhaps the greatest shock. Don Ki-Otah had read our walls, the dust at our feet, and had discerned that which we would not notice in a hundred years. In that way he taught us that there is a secret reality around us all the time. This secret reality reveals all things.

There still remains some doubt as to whether his reading of this secret reality is a consequence of his madness, or whether our inability to read it is a consequence of our dimness. It may just be that we are blind to the prophecies written on the plain features of our times.

That day, after he returned the printed pages to me, he cast one last look at the workshop. Did ever a glance reveal the poverty and richness of a place? For a moment, seeing it through his eyes, I wanted to tear down every brick from that squalid workshop. But then, seeing it through his eyes the next moment, I glimpsed an unsuspected magnificence. With his unique seeing he could transform a hovel into a palace, and a palace into a hovel.

After that ambiguous gaze, he turned to me. I expected from him a long speech, such as antique knights are inclined to give. I braced myself for meandering locutions. Instead he favored me with a smile, in which was mixed compassion and amusement. To this day I have not been able to fathom the full meaning of that smile. It bothers me often on the margins of sleep.

With a gesture to Sancho, he left the room. I should write that line twice. No one has ever left a room the way he did. He left it altered forever. He left the room, but the room retained the stamp and magic and chaos of his spirit. Afterward when I went to the workshop a little of Don Ki-Otahism invaded my quiet life.

Why else do I write with elegiac cadences of a moment that happened more than forty years ago? I too would have liked to have set out on a steed and taken on the challenges of our times.

Later we heard how he would attack garage boys thinking they were stragglers from Boko Haram, or would defend a prostitute in Ajegunle thinking her a celebrated Yoruba princess, or how he set upon a convoy of soldiers, accusing them of electoral fraud. In the last instance he was beaten within a half inch of his life for his absurd bravery.

These actions have changed in the telling into deeds of heroism that shame our famous activists. His deeds, reimagined by our storytellers, made my days into something a little glorious. The years have been good to him.

When he died, in a hovel on the edge of the ghetto, surrounded by his beloved books, he had only Sancho with him, and a scheming niece. His last words were not remembered. Sancho was too broken by grief to ever speak of them. But over the months word went around of his passing. All the market women he had irritated, all the politicians he had insulted, all the prostitutes he had tried to reform, all the truck pushers he had taunted, all the bus drivers who flinched when they saw him, all formed processions along his street and held long vigils outside his house.

I speak of these things with too much compression. They ought to be a thousand pages in the telling. But these are hurried and heated times. It is a wonder one can tell any story straight.

What happened with the rest of his life has been retold by many people. They are fleas on the back of a free-roaming bull. I only wanted to tell of one moment and its long aftermath. It is by the aftermaths that we most truly judge greatness.

He stepped out of the printing workshop that day and was struck by the muggy light of the Ajegunle sun. Outside stood the scrawniest donkey I had ever seen. It was flea-ridden and refractory. Don Ki-Otah leaped on the donkey's back, and was immediately thrown. He picked himself up and dusted himself down. He turned to us and said: "It seems Sidama does not want to be ridden today."

That donkey was a rangy stubborn thing. It looked as if it didn't think much of its master. Don Ki-Otah kept coaxing it. He spoke to the brute as if it were an intelligent human being. A crowd gathered to watch the strange sight of a man trying to reason with a donkey.

Then something unexpected happened. While Don Ki-Otah was whispering into the donkey's twitching ear, Sancho gave the beast a short solid kick in the rump. After that the donkey became agreeable. Don Ki-Otah looked at us as if to confirm the efficacy of his technique.

"All you have to do is reason with them," he said.

Then he took up the halter, clambered onto the beast, and rode toward the red cloud gathering in the North.

Boko Haram (3)

He stood there in the room with the saw in his hand and a grin on his face. He asked his men to bring the soldier to him. They dragged in the soldier, an officer. He ordered them to hold the prisoner down so his neck was bare.

Then he began sawing through the officer's neck. The officer screamed and fought but they held him down and the man went on sawing. He sawed through the spurts of blood and through the veins and the solid bone of the neck and he sawed all through the broken garbled cry of the officer.

He sawed away steadily, with a calm expression on his sweaty face. Every now and then he looked up and shouted, "God is Great!" Then he resumed sawing.

The officer had struggled, had bled, had slumped, but the man went on sawing. He had blood and gore down the front of his kaftan. The officer's fat dripped from his beard.

His hair was wild under his turban but his eyes shone calmly.

When he had finished sawing, he held up the head of the officer. Twisted roots of veins dripping blood dangled from the head. The eyes were shut and the mouth twisted, the tongue half out, clamped down tight with bared teeth. The man held up the officer's head, as if it were a lamp.

"This is what will happen to you if you dare to come and fight us," he said, grinning, and then spoke for ninety minutes.

When he finished he was still holding up the decapitated head.

"Did you record that?"

"Yes," said the cameraman.

"All of it?"

"Yes."

"Good. Now they will fear us."

He threw the head on a bundle in a corner of the room. Then he had a shower at the back of the shed, and joined his men for prayers.

A Street

Streets harbor secret and public stories. A street has its habits and repetitions. If something significant has happened on a street it will happen again, in new ways.

There are streets where people are prone to accidents, streets where people are inclined to fall in love, suicidal streets. There are streets where people go mad, streets of inspiration, of revelation.

A poet was once walking along the canal on Maida Avenue. He had been writing an epic, with great difficulty. Halfway up the street a leaf falling from a silver birch made him grasp the true nature of his composition. He hurried home and destroyed the epic he had been laboring over for seven years. In its place he composed a haiku.

Many years later another poet was walking down the same street. He had been writing a haiku for five years. Halfway down the canal a bird's nest on the bare branches of a chestnut tree caused him to grasp the true dimensions of his composition. He rushed home and destroyed the haiku he had been struggling with. In its place, over the next seven years, he composed the epic of a nation coming to being out of fire and returning to the trickle of its magical origins.

These events do not appear in history. The histories of such streets are invisible, like underground rivers.

All We Do

A woman is reading a book
In a landscape shaped by history.
A hill rakes the gray horizon.
All we do is story.

Private acts are dramas.
Our public acts are dreams.
Submerged rivers are thoughts,
Our hopes are misted streams.

Beyond form our souls breathe.
Within form our souls sing.
Mystery belongs to being
Story belongs to the living.

Within this slice of eternity,
We yield to time our story-making sense.
Awake in dreams, we live out myths.
It's what makes us immense.

Acknowledgments

I wish to say thank you to the following people: to my agent Georgina Capel; to the inimitable Anthony Cheetham; to my American editor, Ibrahim Ahmad, and to all the fine people at Akashic Books.

"Prayer for the Living" was originally published as "A Prayer from the Living" in the *Guardian Magazine* in 1993.

"A Sinister Perfection" was first published in *Callaloo* in 2015.

"Ancient Ties of Karma" was first published in *Callaloo* in 2015.

"Mysteries" was first published in the *Sunday Times Magazine* in 2009.

"Tulips" was first published in the newspaper catalog *Turkish Tulips* in 2017.

"The Lie" was first delivered at the Italian literary festival La Milanesiana in 2012 and first published by the *Sunday Times* in 2011.

"Alternative Realities Are True" was originally broadcast as "The Multiverse Murders" with Audible in 2018.

"The Story in the Next Room" was first published in the booklet *The Mystery Feast* in 2015.

"The Overtaker" was first published in the *Daily Mail* magazine.

"Raft" first appeared in the booklet *The Waters of Humanity*, published by CCCB, Barcelona, in 2019.

"Don Ki-Otah and the Ambiguity of Reading" originally appeared as "Don Quixote and the Ambiguity of Reading" in the anthology *Lunatics, Lovers and Poets: Twelve Stories After Cervantes and Shakespeare*, published by And Other Stories in 2016.

"A Street" appeared in a shorter form in the *Shortlist* digital daily *Mr Hyde* in 2016.

"All We Do" was first published in an earlier form in the booklet *The Mystery Feast* in 2015.

Also available by Ben Okri from Akashic Books

The Freedom Artist
336 pages. Hardcover, $30.95 | Paperback, $16.95

"With the stark power of myth, this
political allegory evolves into an
argument for artistic freedom."
—*New York Times Book Review*

"A perfect read for a post-truth era."
—NPR

"The concise, declarative prose and
the parable-like architecture of the stories
resemble ancient forms of wisdom
literature."—*Wall Street Journal*

"Where fiction's master of enchantments stares down a real horror and, without
blinking or flinching, produces a work of beauty, grace, and uncommon power."
—Marlon James, author of *Black Leopard, Red Wolf*

"Man Booker–winner Okri's modern allegory specifies and beautifully renders the
impact on the human spirit when people are deprived of history and truth. Written
with a striking simplicity that belies the significance of its message, Okri's tale is especially resonant in our current post-truth environment."—*Booklist*, starred review

"[H]aunting and inspiring . . . In this story of political abuse and existential angst,
Okri employs a powerful and rare style reminiscent of free verse and evoking a
mythical timbre. This is a vibrantly immediate and penetrating novel of ideas."
—*Publishers Weekly*, starred review